GRASPING THE FUTURE

GRASPING THE FUTURE

P.I.V.O.T. LAB CHRONICLES™ BOOK NINE

MICHAEL ANDERLE

DISRUPTIVE IMAGINATION

Copyright © 2020, 2021 LMBPN Publishing
Cover copyright © LMBPN Publishing
Cover Art by Jake @ J Caleb Design
http://jcalebdesign.com / jcalebdesign@gmail.com
A Michael Anderle Production

LMBPN Publishing
PMB 196, 2540 South Maryland Pkwy
Las Vegas, NV 89109

First US Edition, February, 2021
(Previously published as a part of the Megabook, *No Time To Quit*)
eBook ISBN: 978-1-64971-499-2
Print ISBN: 978-1-64971-500-5

THE GRASPING THE FUTURE TEAM

Thanks to the JIT Readers

Billie Leigh Kellar
Dave Hicks
Deb Mader
Diane L. Smith
Jeff Eaton
Jeff Goode
John Ashmore
Kelly O'Donnell
Kerry Mortimer

If I've missed anyone, please let me know!

Editor
The Skyhunter Editing Team

CHAPTER ONE

"Hey, man." Nick came into the conference room balancing a precarious stack of sandwiches. "I brought you lunch."

Ben's stomach rumbled. "Argh. I wish I could, but...they're putting me under again today and it means no eating for a while beforehand."

"I'm sorry. I'll get these out of your vicinity, then." He looked at the now-closed door and made one attempt to open it with his elbow before he stepped back and swung a foot up to press on the door handle.

"I'll help you." Ben stood up and the usual mismatch of ability and coordination resulted. When he hit the table with his legs, he sighed.

He had progressed significantly from where he'd been immediately after the climbing accident, but his coordination was still far from where he instinctively thought it was. During his recovery, he had spent hundreds of hours within the virtual reality world of PIVOT to strengthen his muscles and work on fine motor control. What he had achieved there was a good indication of what he could still achieve in the real world.

It would merely take time.

Despite his initial clumsiness, he moved his hand onto the door handle on the first attempt. When he watched his fingers, it was easier to close them around the metal and push it down. Then, he had to back away and pull the door open at the same time, which entailed a fair number of motions he had to accomplish simultaneously.

Predictably, he hit himself on the head with the door more than once. It was good, he thought, that Prima wasn't there to see him.

"Thanks," Nick said when it was finally open. Politely, he didn't mention anything about his lack of coordination. "I'll be back in a few, okay?"

"Sure," he said. He wasn't quite sure why the PIVOT engineer would want to talk to him, but there had been such a constant stream of medical evaluations that he'd probably forgotten about one of the follow-ups.

Ben hobbled to the desk to glance at the job summaries he'd worked through yet again before Nick returned. After getting his PhD in Chemistry, he had been unwilling to play the political and research funding games of academia and had disdained corporate jobs.

He hadn't considered military or defense work. His outlook on military action had been that war movies were sometimes cool to watch but that running people into each other in a war of attrition was a stupid idea. He hadn't understood why people would sign up to be on the ground for those conflicts, and he hadn't been interested in discovering why either.

That outlook was one of many things that had changed in the past few weeks. Confronted by enemies who were determined to use violence, he had learned that sometimes, there was no way to avoid a war of attrition. He had learned to strike quickly and decisively.

And, by doing that, he had learned that you needed to do your research first. If you were blinded by a desire for vengeance—or even by a desire for justice—you could cause harm to innocent people.

Ben had known for a long time that you couldn't control what the world threw at you. What he had failed to appreciate was that situations weren't take-it-or-leave-it. He had always been an or-leave-it kind of guy who sparked fights with a hard-headed and brutally honest approach and then ran when things blew up.

Now, he was willing to de-escalate, defuse…and stay.

You couldn't change things if you weren't there to fight for them.

As a result, he now took a second look at a number of things. From jobs to relationships, he was constantly in new territory. His treatment at the PIVOT Labs had been funded by their parent company, Diatek, a major player in defense contracting. Anna Price, the CEO of Diatek, had looked at Ben's resume while he was inside the virtual world and had decided to send him job openings she'd found.

As a thank you, he tried to give them a fair study and assessment.

He looked up when Nick came in. "Hey."

"Hi." The man stood in the doorway. "I forgot to ask if you wanted any company. I saw you sitting here in the dark, and…" He shrugged.

"I could use a break, honestly."

"Do you want to go outside? It smells like cigarettes and pee but it is fresh air. Allegedly."

"First, don't go into advertising." Ben laughed despite himself. "And no, but not because of the smoke. I merely don't want to smell food."

"I can understand that." Nick came in and sat. "Are you looking at job openings?

"Yeah. Apparently, that's a thing." He rubbed his head. "I can't tell you how grateful I am to all of you that this treatment is being covered, that I'm not being…bankrupted. Not that I had anything for them to take. Blood from a stone. But when this is over, I'll need to go back to the real world and that's…"

The engineer nodded and leaned back in his chair. Ben at first thought he was ignoring him, then realized that he was thinking.

"I think the 'real world' is kind of a made-up concept," he said finally.

"Oh? Do tell." He started—purely out of habit—his series of hand exercises. To someone who didn't know what he'd been through, he looked like he was compulsively tapping his fingers on the table in a specific, staccato rhythm. The movements were still jerky but each day, he grew closer to doing them smoothly without looking at them.

"Yeah." Nick slouched in his chair and looked at him. "Have you ever noticed that when people say, 'you have to learn how to live in the real world,' they aren't talking about the world. They're talking about a specific compromise they had to make or a dream they gave up?"

"I—holy shit." Ben's fingers stopped moving. "Holy shit, I hadn't noticed that. Huh."

"Yeah." The engineer gave him a gleam of a smile. "So I guess my point is, Jacob and Amber and I have lived the dirt-poor life-style, we've faced jail time for this, we worked out of this teeny tiny lab that we came in on the weekends to clean ourselves, and now, we have a shiny new lab and assistants. But even when things were grim, we weren't living in the 'real world' everyone talked about because we were still trying to make this work."

He frowned. "Wait, hold up—jail time?"

"Ohhh." Nick sighed, then looked panicked. "I don't want you to think we were being shady or anything. Also, I'm not sure I'm legally able to talk about it. Very long story short, PIVOT is a treatment that could take some market share and it turns out that people get nasty when profits are on the line."

Ben shook his head.

"It's fine, we have lawyers now." The man shrugged. "The

point is, when you think of the real world, what do you think about? What's the concession you think you have to make?"

"Working a job I hate," he said. "Settling down somewhere, the same old thing every day, and stupid fights with coworkers that drag out for years. Work that doesn't...do anything."

"There you go." Nick spread his hands. "That's not merely an objective look at the real world, it's a set of concessions you don't want to make in your life. So how do you make sure you don't do the same old thing every day? It sounds like it could be consultant work or something—you know, traveling, meeting new coworkers, working on new projects. Or maybe you *do* work the same job but you travel every month. You see?"

"I do." Ben started his finger exercises again. "Okay, yeah." He looked at the jobs and blew a breath out. "I think part of it is... all that stuff I don't like, what if I needed to do it because the organization did good stuff—necessary stuff someone had to do?"

"Ah, now you come to an actual dilemma." The engineer grinned at him. "And I have my opinions on the matter but I'll keep my mouth shut."

"Oh?"

"It's uncharacteristic, I know. I've been informed that I'm the 'nosy old biddy' of the team, and it's a responsibility I take seriously but sometimes, you have to let the young solve their own problems." He mimed being old.

"How very wise of you," Ben said and snickered.

"I think so," Nick said peaceably. "Should we get you ready to go into the game?"

He checked the clock. "Probably."

"Your coordination is certainly improving. You looked up exactly to where you wanted to and then back down."

"I did, didn't I? Huh." Ben gathered the papers, a process that was decidedly less graceful than his glance at the clock. He managed to get all of them into a folder—admittedly, not all facing the same way—and stood. "So you haven't heard from the doctor yet about exact program specifications?"

"Not yet. I get the sense that two PTs are hashing something out."

"So, two experts can't agree on how to proceed," he said. "That's comforting."

"They might agree and they're simply fine-tuning," the engineer told him. "Don't leap to negative conclusions."

"I'll do what I want," he told him.

"Of course you will." Nick held open the door with a grin.

The two men progressed slowly down the hallway. The lab was, as always, buzzing with activity. There were several patients in the pods at present, almost all of them individuals who had been chosen to gain an idea of baseline physical reactivity to the virtual reality.

Two others seemed to be something different and multiple people monitored the feeds at all times. He wasn't quite sure what the situation was there, but no one seemed particularly panicked so he wasn't worried.

Near his pod, Dr. DuBois and Jacob were deep in discussion. When they saw the two men, they waved them over.

"How are you feeling?" Jacob asked Ben.

"Hungry."

"Okay, then let's get you into the pod." The man checked his watch. "No food since last night, right?"

"Yes," he said plaintively.

"Then, I'd say we're good to go. Come this way and we'll get you changed and prepped."

Thirty interminable minutes of prep later, he lay in the pod. It was difficult to feel comfortable with a feeding tube and multiple monitors, but he was already sliding out of this reality. He watched Nick counting down with his fingers and smiled.

The instant transition to freezing cold and wet was abrupt and jarring.

"What the *fuck?*"

"It's good to see you again, too," Prima said.

Ben wrapped his arms around his head to try to avoid the rain somewhat, but there was no good way to do that. The wind gusted in multiple directions and he got drenched no matter how he stood. It might be dusk or dawn, as there was a certain amount of light behind the leaden clouds, but there wasn't much light and the rain didn't do him any favors.

He turned slowly to study his surroundings. A forest behind him was surprisingly dark and made noises he could hear even over the rain. He stood on a road, which meant he might get somewhere by going in one direction or another, and in the distance...lights, he realized

With no point in waiting, he set off. His shirt was soaked through and stuck to his body, his cloak did do not a damned thing for him, and his boots were filling with water.

Prima, he thought, was probably enjoying the hell out of this.

"Tell me that's an inn."

"It is indeed an inn. The one Orien mentioned to you."

"If I recall, he also said it barely deserved the name."

"He did. And he was correct."

"Great." he sighed. "Well, as long as it's warm and dry."

"You'll be disappointed."

"You have to be kidding me. No? Seriously, fuck this." Ben wrapped his cloak a little tighter—why, he wasn't sure—and struggled onward.

CHAPTER TWO

Initially, coming from the isolated island and into the rest of the PIVOT world was exciting. Caravans sometimes passed Jamie and Taigan. The cavalcades kept to themselves, however, and made a point of emphasizing the weapons carried by their guards.

It took them a while to realize that they were worried about a robbery.

"Do we seriously look like competent robbers?" she demanded and frowned at her brother.

"Nope," he said after a moment of thought. "Only nope for me but certainly nope for you. My clothing is halfway respectable. Yours is…a burlap sack?"

"Well, *excuse me*, Mr. I Have A Belt Over My Burlap Sack." She rolled her eyes. "I wouldn't mind a more comfortable set of clothes, though. And a bath. Are there baths here?"

"I don't know. Maybe? Prima?"

"There are baths here. Why wouldn't there be?"

"Well, I always woke up clean so baths didn't seem necessary," the girl pointed out.

"Ah. Right."

After a pause, an icon appeared in front of them on the road. It was the size of a full-length mirror and displayed her in a much better selection of clothes.

"See if you can make these for yourself," Prima said.

"Uh…" Taigan looked at Jamie.

"She never had me do this," he replied.

"Right." She looked at the clothes, then at herself. While she could picture the garments, she couldn't seem to replace those she presently wore. She tried to think about how it would feel to wear the new ones, which looked much softer, and got nowhere. "Prima, I don't think—"

Jamie disappeared and the world took on a bluish hue.

"Dammit," she said. "I world-shifted again, didn't I?"

"Yes." Prima neither explained nor elaborated.

"Bah. Well, if I'm not going to be in the *real* world…" Taigan dressed in a sweeping gown of blue silk. After a second's thought, she added a necklace of fist-sized diamonds and swept her hair into a pile on top of her head. "Yes, hello, I am Princess Taigan of —ooooh, can I have a sword down my back like Wonder Woman did?" One appeared, nestled between her shoulder blades, and she craned to look over her shoulder. "Aww, yeah. I'm badass and —oh, hey, Jamie."

Her brother stared at her, his jaw hanging.

"What?" She looked at the dress. "Oh, right."

"You, uh…" He cleared his throat. "I don't think you can appreciate how much seeing you in a dress cut down to *there* is *bumming me out.*"

"Don't be such a baby," she retorted.

"Oh, yeah? Then maybe I'll wander around shirtless. Or…in a banana hammock."

"Ew, no, stop!"

"I'll do it." Jamie jabbed a finger at her. "Get a dress with a front, or so help me—"

"All right, all right!" He disappeared in the next moment and she changed her clothes hastily. It was a bummer about the sword in the back of the dress, she thought. She had liked that part.

The diamonds, not so much. It turned out that they were big and heavy. She also changed her hair into a French braid and took a few moments to replace her boots with some she liked.

"Cool," she said, when she was done and world-shifted again to see Jamie.

"I wish you wouldn't do that," he said in annoyance. "I'm always worried you won't come back."

"I know, but I don't seem to be able to summon things here. How did you learn?"

"I can't summon things." Jamie looked at her. "Wait, when you world-shift—does Prima not make those outfits?"

"No. It's like in the first part of the world—how you simply summon yourself a bed, or food, or whatever." Taigan frowned at his dumbstruck expression. "You didn't do that part?"

"No. No, I did not."

A throat cleared and they waited for the AI to speak. *"It isn't... precisely...normal,"* she admitted. *"Taigan is the only one I've seen who can do it. It is intriguing that she retains the ability but not within the same game world. Of course...well, never mind."*

"No, no." He shook his head. "Tell us what you were going to say."

His sister nodded.

"I intended to say that in the other world, I had specifically thought I was not continuing an instanced version of this zone. Taigan seems to have made one of those too when she shifted."

"Huh." The girl considered this. "Do you think I could do this during, like...a battle?"

"I haven't the faintest idea. However, I would advise extreme caution. Dying in this game is difficult for the body in the real world. With a healthy human, it is merely unpleasant. However, when one is already experiencing a health crisis, there could be complications."

"Complications like *what?*" Taigan demanded. Prima didn't

answer at once and she looked at Jamie. "Did they tell you about this when they put me in here? Prima, complications like *what*?"

"Up to and including death," the AI conceded finally.

"And you didn't *tell* me?" she demanded and waved her arms indignantly. "No, no, no. I will not do this. You had me in here for *weeks* and you never told me that if I died here, I could physically die?"

"Until very recently, there were explicit blocks in the game that would prevent anything like that from happening."

Jamie, who had studied the area as if he searched for Prima's server and planned to set fire to it, looked up with interest. "Really?"

"Yes. In the blue zone Taigan first encountered, as well as the forest and the original grasslands, there was no way for her to be injured. There were protocols in place to shield her in ways her mind would process as safety. In the most recent zone, the same type of controls were in place but only after a certain amount of damage."

"But *now*," Taigan said, "I could die. That's what you're telling me."

"Yes. Unfortunately, as you saw from the progress you made while under threat of danger, the response of the sympathetic nervous system is critical to the process."

"Great." She rolled her eyes and started walking.

"Where are you going?" her brother called after her.

"I don't know!" she responded. "I don't have a plan. I only want to get the fuck out of here."

She walked without paying attention to where she was going while the sky grew slowly darker and rain began to spatter around her. Taigan held a palm out to feel the rain, shook her head at the weather, and continued. Jamie was behind her, walking quietly and occasionally muttering to Prima, but neither of them tried to talk to her.

Within a few minutes, the rain progressed from a sprinkle to heavy drops that spattered across her face and clothes. She had no idea where she was by now and her feet ached. The foliage around them had grown from sparse vegetation to a real forest, and between the rain and the fading daylight, she was barely able to see the road.

The weather was also loud enough to make it hard to hear anything, something they discovered when they almost ran into an animal on the road.

"Animal" was a generous term. The beast reached almost to Taigan's ribs at the shoulder. Shaggy fur seemed reminiscent of a wolf and there was a tail, but whether it was a wolf, a large cat of some kind, or even a bear, she could not have said.

She jumped and it mirrored her before it backed away quietly, its tail lashing, and crouched. A growl built slowly in its throat.

"Seriously?" she yelled at the sky. "Are you *kidding* me with this? First, you tell me I can die here, then you send this *thing* to —fuck!!"

The creature leapt at her and she threw herself out of the way. Unfortunately, to judge by the scream from behind her, Jamie had not anticipated either meeting it or the swift attack.

Also unfortunately, the road had become slick, muddy, and still very uncomfortable to land on. She scrambled to her feet. "Jamie!"

He was on his back and the animal snapped at his face while he held its jaw away from him.

She yanked her staff out —while she still hankered after the sword, a staff was probably good—and brought it down on the animal's back once, twice, and three times. "Get off him!"

Its head whipped around and it snarled. She stabbed her weapon forward and landed a blow to its mouth and teeth. Its muscles bunched and it staggered away, but not before Jamie howled in pain.

"Jamie!" Taigan skidded to her knees beside him in the dark. "Where—"

"I'm…I'm fine." He took her hand. "Get me up."

"But—"

"We *won't* be fine if we don't get rid of this monster," he told her.

She couldn't argue with that so started to help him up, then shoved him down again as the animal hurtled overhead. Jamie grunted in pain but she couldn't afford to focus on that. When she hauled him up, she still couldn't make out any bloodstains as it was dark.

The girl told herself firmly that she had to stop thinking about it. She snatched the staff up and turned. Where was the damned monster?

A gleam of eyes betrayed its location. Taigan slashed and drove forward with a yell. "Get away!" she shouted. "Go back into the woods and find somewhere dry and *stay* there!"

Her brother might be injured but he was still fast. While she held the animal's attention, he circled and it backed into a sword thrust. It howled and he made a noise that sounded like he was trying not to scream in pain.

"Can you do another hit?" she called.

"I don't think…no, I can't. I'm sorry, I'm so—"

"Aaaaaaaaah!" She attacked the animal with a shriek. Bleeding, it whipped its head around and tried to decide where to run.

Taigan began to whack it with the staff with no attempt at strategy. She merely wanted to land as many blows as possible and as hard as possible. She had no idea how many times you had to batter something with a stick to make it die, but she assumed she was about to find out.

The head and the spine originally seemed like good targets, but every time she landed a strike there, the staff shuddered and her palms ached. She began to hiss through her teeth with every blow, then returned to yelling bloody murder.

It relieved the pain somewhat.

"Get! Away! From! My! Brother!" She punctuated each word with a swing of the staff.

The animal backed away and hissed viciously as it swung its head and looked for an opening.

"Taigan, it's going to jump!"

"I know!"

She pushed it to the very last moment, even though she knew she ran the risk of razor-sharp cat teeth to the face. The problem was that being this angry made it difficult to care about that. The chance of landing another blow was too seductive to waste. One hit, and another, and—

Jamie tackled her sideways. The creature sailed overhead and landed heavily over them and he wrapped his sister's hand around the hilt of his sword.

"Kill it!" he said.

Taigan stabbed upward with all her might and the beast howled. Blood began to pour out of its mouth and its eyes changed.

A grimy woman collapsed on top of her, her eyes wide and staring and her body limp.

"Ew! *Ew!*" She pushed her away and scrambled to her feet. "Holy…shit…fucking—" She stared at the human body in the road, recalled the staring eyes, and stumbled to the forest's edge to lose her lunch at high velocity.

"Taigan?" Jamie asked tentatively.

"Yeah?"

"Are you injured?"

"No." She edged cautiously to where he stood. "You?"

"Kinda." One hand was pressed over the other shoulder. "Who the hell is this?"

"I don't know." She forced herself to kneel next to the body. The clothing barely deserved the name. It was dirty, stinking, and several shades *worse* than her burlap sack.

There was no rational explanation.

"What's that?" She pointed when something caught her eye.

"What's what? I can't—oh, I shouldn't kneel. Just tell me."

Taigan peered closely at it. "It's a gold ring. Like, real gold."

Jamie staggered.

"Hey, whoa." She stood to support him. "Okay, let's find some-place with a doctor."

"What about the ring?" he mumbled.

She looked at the body. The ring was probably valuable. It looked simple too. But something about the difference between the gold ring and the grimy clothes, the monstrous animal, and the gaunt human, made her break out in a cold sweat.

"We don't want to touch that," she said decisively. "Do you have your sword? Good. Okay, let's get you somewhere safe. Come on."

CHAPTER THREE

The town Ben finally reached was little more than a collection of buildings. In the same way, the inn was less the type of cozy tavern from fantasy books and more a drafty building that smelled of both mildew and stale beer. And, predictably, a few other things he didn't want to think about it.

The lights inside seemed bright when he first stepped in out of the rain, but they were hidden behind soot-covered glass and provided neither warmth nor stable light. The same could be said for the fire in the hearth, which sputtered and frequently guttered low when the wind gusted outside.

The few patrons were clustered around its feeble warmth when he walked in. He saw them study the make of his cloak and the hilt of the sword and come to certain conclusions.

While he wasn't sure which conclusions those were, he had zero intention to make himself a target. He leaned over the tiny counter to peer into the kitchen and located the innkeeper seated in a chair, drinking from a filthy mug of ale.

"Eh?" The man stood and wiped his beard.

"Ale and food," he said. In all honesty, he didn't want either from this establishment, but he needed something and this was evidently the best he could hope to find. He made sure to not flash any coins that the men at the fireplace could see and found a seat in the corner.

The seat was sticky enough that he judged it better to sit on his sodden cloak than directly on the chair.

The food, when it arrived, was unappetizing shades of brown with various lumps. Ben stared at it, prayed he couldn't get food poisoning in this world, and began to eat as fast as was humanly possible.

It tasted good, which was somehow even more unnerving.

He had barely finished when the door banged open and two figures entered. Both were so tall and slim that he originally mistook them for elves, especially with their black hair and deathly-pale skin. When the features resolved in the dim lighting, he registered two shockingly young individuals, a boy and a girl who could only be siblings.

She levered her brother into a seat and gasped when she saw something on his shirt that from where Ben sat seemed to be the red of blood. When she whispered something, the boy shook his head, but she looked around defiantly and drew a breath to call for a healer.

Her words froze in her throat when she saw who was around. The men at the fireplace looked at the two youngsters with contempt and open assessment, and the innkeeper hadn't come out from behind the counter. Her clothes were good enough, but neither of them looked rich.

No coin purses were visible.

He leaned back to watch the unfolding scene. The girl fixed the room with a glare that said she was prepared to off the first person to say anything, then strode to the innkeeper. She said something quietly and he made an easily recognizable gesture, rubbing the tips of his thumb and fingers together.

She deflated visibly, gave him a blazing look, and returned to her brother's side.

Ben's mind churned although he remained outwardly neutral. The men at the fireplace now whispered to one another, and he had a sudden idea. He brought his mug to the counter for wine and stayed while the innkeeper poured. When the man returned, he slid a coin across the counter for him.

"The gentlemen at the fire," he said casually. "Buy them all a round on me, eh?"

The proprietor looked intrigued. "I could do that."

"I'd like them to have a good night," he said meaningfully. "Have a good few drinks and go home." His gaze moved to indicate the young woman and her brother. "Rather than doing anything they might regret," he said meaningfully.

The innkeeper paused. "Ah," he said finally. He hesitated, but whether it was greed or the desire for an evening with a fight, he took the coin and retrieved some mugs from the ceiling, giving Ben a nod.

He returned to his seat and waited as the man brought the ale to the men at the fire. Whatever he said was brief, but they looked over their shoulders at him. He met a few gazes, careful to not make it a battle of wills, but raised his mug once to them in a toast. A couple toasted him warily in response.

Not long after that, they finished their drinks and left. He watched them go, sipped his ale, and waited to see if they would return. It was a little tiresome as he wasn't good at waiting. He wanted to go to the siblings immediately. Patience, however, had encouraged the men to leave without a fight, and he was ready to put in the same patience now if need be.

The men did not return.

He flipped another coin to the innkeeper. "Food and ale for those two," he said as he stood. "And is there a healer?"

"Aye." The man smiled grimly. "My wife would tend a wolf if it came in bloody. I have t' be careful to keep her from taking in too many strays."

"I'll pay for these two," he said easily.

The proprietor disappeared and Ben went to the table with the siblings.

The girl looked at him as he sat. He knew her glare was the only thing she had right now, but it was impressive nonetheless. It said she wasn't afraid to use the staff she'd leaned up against the wall behind her.

"Food and ale are coming," he said. "A healer, too."

The boy looked up, his eyes hazy with pain and hope, but his sister's face didn't clear at all.

"Who are you?" she demanded.

"A traveler, nothing more."

She wanted to send him away, he could see that. Her instinct was to tell him to get lost and she would have if her brother hadn't winced slightly beside her. She turned her head quickly and bit her lip as she looked at him.

"About a week ago, I was a stray on the streets of Heffog," Ben said. "An elf took me in and nursed me back to health. Let's say I'm paying it forward."

Her wariness eased but only slightly. When the innkeeper returned with bowls of the brown, lumpy food, she muttered her thanks and nodded before she looked at the bowl.

He leaned forward and darted a glance at the proprietor, who lingered near the counter and pretended not to watch them. "A word of advice," he said quietly. "It tastes good but don't look at it too hard."

The boy managed a laugh before he winced again, and even the girl looked more at ease. They began to eat with the incredible speed of growing teenagers and had both finished their food by the time the innkeeper's wife appeared.

The woman clucked over their empty bowls and yelled something into the kitchen. Ben didn't speak the local dialect but he didn't need to. He'd known enough grandmothers to be sure that her words were some variant of, "These children look like they're about to snap in half. Give them more food right now."

While the innkeeper approached with more dollops of stew and a long-suffering sigh, his wife pushed the boy's shirt back and began to clean his injury. The shockingly deep puncture wound looked ugly.

However grandmotherly the woman was, she didn't pull her punches when it came to cleaning the wound or wrapping it. The boy yelped more than once and even came out of his chair, only to be pushed down again. She smeared ointment in the injury and bound it with clean bandages.

It was a total mystery how she kept them clean when the rest of the inn was so dirty.

"Rest," she instructed the boy firmly in accented English. "A week of rest. Listen?"

It took Ben a moment to realize that she was asking if he understood. The boy, whether he understood or not, nodded.

"Tea," the woman said and disappeared into the other room without another word.

The girl looked at their benefactor. "Who are you?" she asked again. "No one does something for nothing."

He hesitated. "I'm Ben," he said finally. "I'm...well. Are you from here, the two of you?" When her expression became a little speculative, he asked, "Or are you dreaming from a white pod in New York?"

"Oh!" Her eyes lit up. "Yes. Both of us."

"Taigan," the boy managed and winced.

"Shh." She made a gesture at him as the innkeeper's wife appeared with a big bowl of tea that smelled vile.

The four of them stared at one another. The woman was waiting for the boy to drink it, clearly without the intention of leaving until he did, and neither Taigan nor Ben was brave enough to intervene.

The hapless patient glared at them before he gulped the tea. From the look on his face, it was far less pleasant than the stew, but he managed to hold in his gagging until the woman left again.

"That was so bad," he managed finally. His eyes rolled up in his head and his head thunked down on the table.

"Jamie!"

"He's all right," Prima said. From the way both Taigan and Ben moved their heads, they could tell that the other one was listening. *"There was a herb in the tea for sleeping."*

"So now we have to haul him upstairs?" the girl asked.

"Yes."

"Of course," Ben muttered. "And you'll laugh at us while we do, won't you?"

"I think you know the answer to that."

"Yeah, well." The girl looked venomously at the ceiling. "You got Jamie attacked by a fucking bear-cat monster. You can laugh, but if I ever find you, I'm gonna kick some *ass*."

Prima wisely said nothing to that.

Getting the boy upstairs was an ungainly process. Two rooms had been made ready, one with two beds separated by a sheet and one with one little bed. They each had another soot-streaked lantern and both were even draftier than the downstairs area.

He resigned himself to the fact that he wouldn't dry out until he left. Once he'd helped to wrestle the boy into bed, he nodded at Taigan.

"I'll see you tomorrow?"

"I…think so." She shrugged.

"He's all right," Ben told her. "Prima wouldn't let him get hurt. Not really."

"That's what *you* think," she said resentfully.

He was going to ask what that meant but saw how exhausted she was.

"Get some sleep," he suggested. "Food and sleep won't make this place less damp, but they'll make things easier to deal with. We can come up with a plan for you two tomorrow."

She hesitated, then nodded and ran a hand through her bedraggled hair. "Thanks," she told him.

"Sure." He went into his room and closed the door before he said to Prima, "What's she mad about?"

"Mmm. I'll let her tell you."

"You realize that will paint a less flattering portrait of the situation than you'd give me yourself?"

"I hadn't thought of that. Humans are sneaky. Nonetheless, it isn't my story to tell."

It was an interesting statement. He considered what it might entail but was suddenly so tired that he could barely pull his cloak and boots off before he fell onto the bed. His last thought before he fell asleep was to wonder if there had been herbs in the stew, too.

CHAPTER FOUR

Taigan woke to sunlight streaming through the windows.

That was her first thought but instead, it soon became clear that she had woken to sunlight streaming through the gaps in the wall. She looked at the still-damp boards and shook her head.

No sounds came from Jamie's side of the sheet. She stood carefully and tiptoed around the edge of it. He slept peacefully with deep, even breaths, and his face had good color.

She wasn't trained as a doctor, but that seemed positive. She crept closer, held her hand above his forehead to see how warm it was, and craned forward to peer at his shoulder. The cat-creature must have used him as a launch point after the first attack.

Although she couldn't see the wound, no lines extended from it and the area didn't seem to be red or hot. That also seemed positive.

He didn't so much as stir while she examined him, which led her to believe that he was still drugged to high heaven. Jamie was, otherwise, a fairly fussy sleeper. She returned to her side of the sheet and tried to decide what to do.

Now that she was up, she could hear people moving downstairs and even footsteps coming past in the hallway. Ben, maybe? This seemed a fairly out of the way place so it was probably him.

She washed awkwardly with the ewer of water and a damp cloth, briefly pondered the fact that she would sell her soul for antiperspirant, and checked again to see if her brother was still asleep. When she confirmed that he was, she took a deep breath, closed her eyes, and let the world dissolve around her.

In her other plane of existence, it was no trouble to clean up and re-braid her hair. Taigan made herself another set of clothing and returned to the game world. She had improved with this, although she couldn't seem to stop holding her breath when she did it like she was plunging into a pool.

Well, everyone had their quirks. She disappeared into the ether once more and came back with a note that said *DOWN-STAIRS -T*, which she placed on the floor between Jamie's bed and the door. Finally, she crept out and down the stairs.

Ben wasn't up and about yet, but the innkeeper's wife was. She fussed around the girl and brought her porridge with a lump of butter and a thick dollop of what turned out to be maple syrup. Taigan usually wasn't much of a one for overly sweet foods, but it turned out that near-death experiences had quite an effect on her appetite.

She was almost finished when Ben came down the stairs. He looked around for Jamie.

"He's not up yet," she said. "He seems to be recovering well."

"Good." He sat and looked for the innkeeper. "What's on the menu? There's not enough left in your bowl for me to tell what it was."

Taigan flushed. "Porridge stuff. It's good. And it looks better than the stew."

"Yeah, that didn't take much." He frowned at her. "So, do you want to tell me what two teenagers are doing here...in fairly desperate straits?"

"Oh." She waited while the innkeeper's wife came and set a bowl of porridge down. From the serving size, she seemed to have decided that he was worthy of the best as he'd paid for Jamie to be treated.

The girl waited while he took a mouthful and nodded in pleasure.

"It's good, right?"

He made a muffled sound of agreement.

"So, I'm in a coma," Taigan said.

Ben choked on his food and gave her a sharp look.

She shrugged. "It happens sometimes."

"I know that, but it's still…what happened?"

"Oh, I mean it simply happens to me sometimes. It's happened since I was little. I fall into a coma and then I'm in one for a while. No one knows why. But Jamie—he's my twin—heard about this project and he got us into it. We've been in a different part of the game until now, and we're only…getting into the normal part." She sighed. "I'm not sure I like it."

"No?" He gave her a smile that said he understood all too well. "I haven't been a fan of everything I've seen either. It's kind of like the real world, huh?"

"I suppose." She curled her legs up. "I beat a cat-whatever to death with a staff last night. Mostly. Then I stabbed it."

"Sure."

"I didn't like that. Especially because—" Taigan suddenly remembered everything in a rush. With Jamie's injury and the darkness and fear, she hadn't focused on what had happened. She leaned closer to Ben. "The creature that attacked us—the cat, I mean—it was a person, a woman. She transformed into a human when I killed her and she had this ring…"

Ben, sipping something that looked like tea but smelled like hot ale, raised his eyebrows. "Ring?"

"A gold ring. But she was so poor that she was starving to death. She would have sold it, I'd think." She shivered. "I think it had something to do with her being a cat. Does this world work this way?"

"This world works in many ways," he said, his tone a little disgruntled. "Not all of them are nice. Or fair. Again...like the real world."

"Hmm." She considered that and looked up when she caught a flash of movement from the corner of her eye. "You're up! Should you be walking?"

"I'm *fine*," Jamie said, clearly prickly. He came down the stairs and to the table, sat close to his sister, and darted a barely disguised glare at her companion.

Ben took another mouthful of his porridge to hide a smile before he said, "I'll go tell the innkeeper you're here for breakfast."

He had barely moved out of sight when Jamie whispered, "What the hell are you doing?"

"Eating breakfast? Talking with the other person from the real world?" Taigan looked at him.

"He's dangerous," her brother said flatly.

"I...okay, back up. How do you know this?"

"You're my sister. I'm supposed to keep you safe."

"Yes," she said patiently, "but how is he dangerous? All he's done is help us. He's here for help exactly like we are. I don't see why we should assume there's a problem."

Jamie glowered in the direction Ben had left in. "You're my sister," he said again.

"Do you...think he's hitting on me?" she asked finally. "Because I honestly don't think he is."

"Are you sure?" he asked.

"I think we're half his age," Taigan protested.

"That doesn't always mean someone's safe."

"Okay, true, but he hasn't been creepy." She sighed at the look on his face. "How about this—if he does anything creepy, my hand to God, I'll stab him."

Jamie's face cleared. "Okay." He held a hand out to shake.

She shook on it. "Just you wait. If we run into a lady somewhere, I'll make you make the same promise."

Ben, with perfect timing, returned with the innkeeper, who held a bowl of porridge. Taigan suspected he had been listening for the optimal time to rejoin them but was unable to confirm her suspicions as he wouldn't meet her eyes.

He certainly *seemed* amused.

"Why are you here?" Jamie asked him when the three of them were alone.

"A climbing accident," the man said. A tenseness stiffened the set of his shoulders. "I lost my ability to move my body—not paralysis. I simply didn't know where my body was at any given time. I've had to learn to walk again and this seems to help." He paused. "Or did you mean why am I in this inn?"

"Both," the boy said after a moment. "Where were you climbing?"

"Colorado." He sighed. "I'm...lucky to be alive. My buddy was also there, and he made it too but he broke a *lot* of bones. I feel guilty about suggesting that route. Anyway, if you're ever in Aspen and you get injured, you should hope you get Dr. Ullmer. She's a miracle worker."

Taigan could see her brother had begun to relax.

"And why are you here in the inn?" she asked.

"Oh, that." He opened his mouth, then closed it. "Um..."

"What?" Jamie asked suspiciously.

"Do you want the good version or the bad version?"

"The good one," she said at the same time her twin said, "The bad one."

"Under a rather obscure section of elvish law," Ben explained, "an elf who is sold into slavery by another elf—of the same nation —is allowed to kill the one who did it. As long as there are seven other elves present. It's complicated. Anyway, I know an elf who had been sold into slavery. He intended to kill the guy who did it to him."

They stared at him, wide-eyed.

"The thing is," he continued, "his immediate heir was someone who would stay in business as a slave trader. His *next* heir was someone who fought for abolition. So...I killed his first heir on the same night. But as you will note, I am not an elf and therefore I needed to get the hell out of there in short order."

A somewhat stunned silence followed.

"So, you murdered someone," Jamie said finally. His voice was flat.

"That's the one," Ben admitted.

"You're not at *all* sorry?" the boy asked incredulously.

Even Taigan was a little unsettled now.

"Oh, I am. I did not want to do that. The thing was, it was necessary, and I couldn't live with myself if I didn't do it." He shrugged. "It's been a hard few weeks here. When I told Taigan that this world wasn't always pretty or fair, I meant it. On the other hand, I think I've become a better person."

"Better person...as in a murderer." Jamie didn't seem inclined to let this go.

His sister had to admit he had a point.

"Yeah," he said. "If it helps, up until I got into the game—and for a while after—I'd have been right there with you."

"I don't think it does help," the boy said after a moment of serious thought.

"Well, that's fair." Ben took a mouthful of porridge. "But it sounds like your sister did some violence last night to save your life and I'd wager you'd do the same for her, right? Or a friend?"

Jamie didn't say anything to that.

"So..." Taigan considered this. "Are you leaving, then?"

"Soon. I'm waiting for someone." He smiled slightly. "Since I needed to leave anyway, I offered to look for my friend's...friend.

Fiancée, I think. She was sold into slavery somewhere out here by the same man and I'll try to track her down."

"And kill her?" the boy muttered into a mouthful of porridge.

She rolled her eyes but knew better than to engage when he had made up his mind about something. He liked to leap to conclusions and then hang onto them for dear life.

He finished his porridge and put his spoon down. "Well, if you're waiting for someone, we should spar."

"*What?*" Taigan and Ben said at the same time.

"You learn who a man is by fighting him."

Ben's face went studiously blank and she winced in empathic embarrassment. Before he could say anything, she hurried to interject.

"That may be, but *you* are on bed rest for one week and I think if you disobey orders, our hostess will make you drink more of that tea."

She had hoped to put the fear of God in her brother, and it looked like she had judged correctly—his eyes went wide.

"There *are* some sparring targets outside," Ben said casually. "I need to practice movement anyway for my physical therapy, so I'll be there if you'd like to join me." He raised an eyebrow at Jamie.

"I can't spar," the boy said grumpily. "Guys, that tea is *so bad*. I can't drink it again."

"It'll at least get you outside," he said. "Come on, both of you."

CHAPTER FIVE

"I'm confused," Prima said as Ben walked through the inn.

"What about?" He kept his voice low so the twins wouldn't hear him. Taigan hung back with her brother, who was running out of energy and did not want to admit it.

"Why doesn't Jamie like you?" she asked. *"I put you all in the same place because I thought you would like each other. It's always worked that way before."*

"Always? Who else have you tried that with?"

"Dotty, Justin, Tina..."

"Yeah, I don't know any of those people. As for Jamie..." He tried to decide how to explain this to her. "He's worried about his sister. He thinks I'll hit on her and make her uncomfortable."

"I'm not always familiar with colloquialisms. 'Hit on' is a euphemism for flirting, yes?"

"Yes." He hid a smile.

"Do you want to flirt with Taigan?"

"I do not." He grinned now. "I'm sure she's a lovely person but she is also a child. I certainly will not flirt with her."

"She is not a child," Prima said after a moment. She was clearly

trying to understand the meaning of his words and seemed to have trouble doing so.

Ben said nothing. If he'd learned anything about the AI, it was that she wanted to learn and advance. He wouldn't give her the answer to her question before she'd had time to puzzle it out.

"*So, humans find age gaps to be disconcerting?*" Prima asked at last.

"Yes," he said patiently.

"*Is it the fact that she is fifty percent of your age or the fact that she is seventeen years younger?*"

"There isn't any hard and fast rule," Ben explained. "It's merely what feels okay at the time. Well...as long as everyone's cool with it and they're adults, which she isn't. Look, this is seriously weird to talk about."

"*I apologize. I am confused. To sum up, Jamie is worried that you will flirt with Taigan, but you do not want to flirt with Taigan?*"

"Yes."

"*Then why don't you simply tell him that?*"

"Oh, you priceless, innocent unicorn." Ben began to laugh and tried to keep his voice low.

"*I am not a unicorn. I am an artificial—*"

"I know. It's another figure of speech. Uh...basically, if I told him that, he wouldn't believe it. Humans lie often. Especially about this kind of thing."

"*You people are exhausting.*"

"It's hard to argue with that," he agreed.

He pushed out into the back yard. The sparring targets he had spoken about were not designed to be targets. Instead, they were old piles of garbage, some of them with the remains of boxes protruding.

The ground was still somewhat wet from the day before but was drying quickly in the day's heat, and Ben took a moment to study the area. Heffog, as Elantria had told him, had the feeling of a city forever in decline. There was a desperate undercurrent to it, the sense that anyone might be watching you and anyone might try to harm you.

This settlement was ramshackle and far from affluent, but it was far more comfortable. You drank your beer, you paid your tab, and in return, everyone obeyed the rules of society.

Taigan and Jamie emerged and looked around for a seat for the wounded boy. A set of barrels stood nearby, filled with God only knew what, but they didn't smell too bad and they would work well for what they needed. He clambered up with Taigan's help, which Ben pretended not to see.

"So," he called over his shoulder as he drew his sword. "You know why I'm here—what's *your* quest?"

"We're supposed to have a quest?" She responded. With a small frown, she moved closer to stare at the piles. "What am I supposed to do with this? It's not exactly...human-shaped."

"Start trying to hit very specific things," he said. "Or try to stop right before hitting them. Basically, anything that gives you more practice in controlling the staff."

"Okay." She sounded doubtful but she took the staff off her back and went to find a pile in another part of the yard.

He didn't talk for a while as he warmed up with the series of passes Zaara had shown him for that purpose. If he did them correctly, the sword hummed through the air. He had no target, not yet. It was simply a series of techniques at all different angles. They forced him to use all the muscles in his arms and core, shift his grasp more than once, and begin using footwork. By the end, he could feel his body awake and ready to go, and he'd had a blessed few minutes with a clear mind—nothing in his head except for the techniques and his muscles.

Ben started into the second set of exercises without looking at the twins. This set was more basic, but Zaara had been adamant that in swordsmanship, as in most areas of life, the basics were what one should spend the most time on.

Now, he let his thoughts run ahead. He was fairly sure that

Prima meant for the twins to accompany him, but he wasn't certain that it would be a good idea. After all, Jamie was injured. If he went into danger—as he suspected he would—the two young people would be vulnerable.

Taigan, of course, had shown that she could handle herself ably. But he had no illusions about whether her brother would be comfortable to remain back at an inn while the two of them went off to fight, as they inevitably would.

On the other hand, he thought as he stepped through for a turn and reverse attack, he couldn't simply leave the two of them there alone. They had no money and not the first idea of where to go to keep themselves safe, and he *certainly* didn't want them to end up in Heffog.

He sighed as he continued.

Taigan looked curiously at him. "Is everything okay?"

Ben nodded wordlessly. She had made short work of two entire piles of garbage and with enough violence that he could absolutely believe she had beaten a cat to death the night before.

She returned to her workout and he moved to where Jamie was seated. He settled himself on a barrel next to the boy and waited for him to speak.

"You stay away from her," Jamie said finally.

He was struck by the very sudden impression that he had become old while he wasn't paying attention. So much was evident in his voice that the boy wasn't aware of. It wasn't only dislike or the threat but the faint self-consciousness and the quaver in the tone that screamed, "I'm not ready for this." And, of course, the uncertainty over whether this was the right thing to do at all. Ben remembered those moments and to his surprise, he felt sympathetic.

"As I recall," he said, as lightly as he could, "she said she would stab me if I tried anything, and I'm gonna go out on a limb and guess she told the truth." He nodded to where Taigan currently destroyed a broken barrel.

Jamie remained silent.

"I expect you'll only believe me as you get to know me," he said. "If you do, I guess. But I have no intention of hitting on her. When the two of you came into the inn last night, you were injured and there were people at the fire looking like they were ready to mug you and I felt...protective. I didn't expect it. I'm only thirty-four. While I know that seems super-old to you, I didn't think I was old enough to feel like I should be taking care of kids."

The boy considered this and finally looked at him. "She's always been falling into these states," he told him. "The comas. I pushed our family to put her in this game. I thought at the start that it had killed her, and I couldn't...that was the worst thing I've ever felt. I wanted to die. It was too much guilt for me to live with. I don't want her to get hurt in here."

Ben looked at him. "Is that what happened with..." He gestured at the wound.

"No." Jamie flushed with embarrassment. "We didn't see the animal until it was too late. It knocked me over and Taigan tried to get it off, and it went to jump and its claws came out." He shuddered at the memory. "God, that moment—I thought it would get my heart. I was so afraid and it hurt *so* much. And then I couldn't help her while she fought it."

He nodded.

"I'm sorry I threatened you," the youngster said finally. "That was uncalled for."

"Eh, I think it's better for Taigan to know her brother has her back," he told him. "So...are we cool?"

"We're cool. Just...you know, if you *do* try something, I won't stop her from stabbing you."

"That's fair." He sighed and looked at the sun. "God, I'm old. You don't think about it until you see someone young."

"What's it like to be...thirty-four?"

"Thank you for not also saying 'old,'" Ben said wryly. "And I hate to tell you, but it's as confusing and weird as being a teenager—only for some reason, you also have to pay bills and take care of yourself. I guess that's the big thing. You still don't know what you're doing."

"Huh." Jamie looked skeptical. He rotated his arm in its socket. "You know, it feels like this is healing." He pulled his shirt aside to look under the bandage. "Oh, shit. Look."

He leaned closer to the boy. What had been a deep and angry red puncture wound was now completely gone.

"What was *in* that salve?" Jamie asked.

"I think it was the tea," he said. "You should probably have more. You know, to make sure."

"New plan," the youngster said, "if you ever hit on my sister, I will make you drink some of that tea."

Ben guffawed.

"What are you two talking about?" Taigan asked suspiciously.

"Jamie's wound is gone," he responded.

"What?" She dropped the staff and ran to them to look. "Holy crap—*how?*"

"I have no idea," her brother told her, "but I'm glad. And I think I will take that sparring match now," he added and looked meaningfully at Ben.

He laughed. "I suppose I earned that. Go easy on the old man, though, will you?"

"Never," Jamie replied cheerfully.

"This isn't a stupid guy thing, is it?" Taigan asked suspiciously. "Because if you two start beating each other, I'll simply leave."

"We're only sparring," the boy promised her.

"And then I'll teach you the warmups I was doing," Ben told him.

"Cool."

The two took their places in the field of scattered debris. Jamie was grinning as he surged forward in an attack.

Ben, however, knew a thing or two about doing foolhardy

charges. He stepped into the charge and saw his opponent's moment of indecision—whether to accelerate his strike or pull up? That indecision cost him as he tapped the boy's ribs lightly with his sword. Jamie winced and swore under his breath but resettled into a fighting stance.

Good. He wouldn't run when he was outmatched. In his experience, that was a critical part of surviving in the world of PIVOT.

This time, Jamie circled and waited. He tried to be careful and feel him out, which was something Ben approved of. The newly discovered old man in him tried to decide whether to give the boy the next point in order to show him that the tactic was good. Most of him, however, felt like he should pull no punches.

He didn't have to decide, as it turned out. As he readied himself to close the gap between them, a bloodcurdling scream came from the front of the inn. The three exchanged panicked looks and all of them sprinted out of the yard and to the road.

CHAPTER SIX

"Whoa, fuck!" Ben skidded abruptly to a stop when he saw what was there. He couldn't stop himself from yelling, but he clapped a hand over his mouth to stifle the noise.

The beast that paced at the front of the inn was mangy and undernourished but no less terrifying for it. He couldn't have said whether it was a wolf or a cat—or, possibly, a bear of some kind. The way it walked was ambiguous. Its paws were gigantic and there were huge claws on each.

Old blood—not new blood, thankfully—was visible on its teeth. Whoever it had scared was presumably in one of the houses by now as there was no sign of blood and no body.

Only an angry wolf-bear-cat paced the empty road. Ben hadn't stifled the sound enough, though, because it looked at the three of them for a long moment as if it tried to decide whether to attack them or not. Its eyes were a sickly yellow-green.

"Oh, crap," Taigan said. "Another one of these fucking things."

"*That's* what you fought the yesterday?" He stared at her, then at Jamie before he looked hastily at the animal.

It, of course, no longer paid attention to them. There was

something insulting about that—it didn't even think they were worth worrying about.

"Well, it was dark," the girl said.

"Yeah, we couldn't see it well," Jamie agreed.

"This is scarier," she finished.

Ben, vividly remembering the dark elf twins he had worked with at Lord Kerill's house, decided to put an end to the ping-pong type of conversation. He waved his hand to quiet them and said firmly, "We need a strategy."

"Operation Rock and a Pointy Place," the twins said immediately in unison.

He stared pointedly at them.

Jamie explained. "Taigan gets its attention and hits it as much as she can with the stick while she drives it back to me so I can kill it. We've practiced it often."

Questions stirred but he filed them to discuss later. "Which side should I be on?"

"You and Taigan be the rock," the boy decided.

"Right." He took a deep breath and looked at her. "Are you ready?"

"Yeah, I guess." She didn't look enthusiastic about this. Still, she readied her grasp on her staff and focused on the beast.

Without warning, she attacked with a battle cry that made Ben want to hide. It took one startled moment before he remembered to follow her.

The monster—he had decided to call it a bear-cat—looked around with a snarl when she raced forward. It crouched, its head whipped from side to side, and it darted sideways around her and launched itself at Ben.

"Fuuuuuuck!" He went over backward and his head struck the cobblestones so hard he saw stars. When he opened his eyes muzzily, he saw a chunk of hit points floating away.

He still seemed to be alive, though, and scrambled to his feet to see Jamie warding the animal off with jabs of his sword. The boy also yelled at random—it seemed to be a family trait—and while their adversary snarled and snapped, it didn't seem willing to get in too close.

Zaara would probably have despaired of the twins, but he had to admit that their balls-to-the-wall-crazy style had definite advantages.

Ben waited until Jamie lunged forward and he timed his strike for when the bear-cat scrambled back, away from the sword. His heavy slash connected successfully with the monster's leg, a little above the knee, and the creature howled. The sound was terrifyingly human.

Then he remembered that, according to Taigan, these things might well *be* human. His stomach turned.

The monster didn't give him time to mull over the morality of the situation. As he had been the first to draw blood, it seemed to have decided he would be the first to die. It bunched into a crouch and launched toward him.

That action was very cat-like. Maybe he would see a full characterization by the time this was over. He decided to think about that while he waited for the right moment—the monster's legs lengthened, the paws left the ground, and its jaws opened—and he ducked and threw himself forward under the animal's trailing feet.

He landed too hard on the cobblestones. This was yet another way in which he was getting old. Things that would have been amusing before were now terrifyingly painful.

"Rock and a pointy place!" Taigan yelled. "Ben, get up!"

"Yeah, yeah." He pushed to his feet beside her. "I think I liked it better when I couldn't move," he said grumpily. "At least then I didn't end up getting myself into these situations."

"This way, however, is more fun for me."

The girl snickered.

"Yes, thank you, Prima." Ben rolled his eyes and looked at her. "Charge?"

"Chaaaarge!" was Taigan's answer.

"They are not subtle, those two," he said to Prima as he followed.

"You're one to talk."

"It takes one to know one, I guess."

To his surprise, the two of them settled into a rhythm fairly quickly. One would dart in with a yell and a few good strikes while the other one prepared and darted in silently to stab at the bear-cat from the opposite side.

All he wanted was for this to be over, but it was difficult to get close enough for a solid blow without the risk of claws or teeth. The creature might have been human to start with, but it had good reach, sharp claws, and dangerous fangs, and it certainly knew how to move.

The thing that kept him going was that it was limping from his first strike. It could be injured. He had done it before and he could do it again.

"Ben, be ready!" Taigan called.

"On it," he responded.

She launched herself closer and spun to put the entire force of her core behind the staff strike. It wasn't fast enough to catch the bear-cat, but he knew that was her purpose. The monster, having to choose between moving carefully or getting out of the way of a bone-crushing blow, reacted on instinct and leapt toward him.

He saw Jamie waving his arms to indicate that he was open. Rather than striking directly at the creature's back, he circled and drove it away from Taigan laterally. Between her strike and his shift of angle, it thought more about evading them than it did about what else might be behind it.

The boy put his whole body into his attack. The bear-cat arched and shrieked. The yellowish-green of its eyes flared and it thrashed and tore the sword from his hand. It stumbled away, clearly in its death throes but still too dangerous to reach. They watched as it sank to the cobbles and its ribs stopped moving.

The shift from monster to human wasn't immediate. The form seemed to melt before their eyes. Patchy fur transformed into tattered clothes, the claws and fangs melted away, and the snout flattened into a human face.

Jamie's sword, however, was still lodged in the man's side.

Ben had recalled Taigan's words about their attacker the night before but half of him had not believed in the transformation. The other half had not appreciated exactly how desperate and emaciated the human was. The cheekbones were gaunt and he could see the line of the ribs even under the shirt.

"Look," Jamie said quietly and pointed at the man's hand.

A gold ring glittered on his finger.

The oddness of it wasn't that it was simply a gold ring on a man who would easily have been desperate enough to sell it. It was the way it glittered, the only thing about him that wasn't dirty. Ben edged closer with the twins beside him.

None of them wanted to touch it.

When he pulled a dagger out and pressed the man's hand down, he saw something else that frightened him.

"Is that..." The boy sounded horrified. "Is it going *into* his hand?"

He had to swallow bile before he could answer. "I think so." The skin around the ring was reddened in a slight but unmistakable pattern. If he had to guess, he would say the ring had spikes on the inside that dug into his flesh.

The wearer couldn't have taken it off without severing his finger. How it had been put on was a mystery.

Suddenly, he remembered why he was there.

"Ben?" Jamie frowned and his expression seemed confused and impatient.

"Orien's friend," Ben said slowly. "She was a *goldsmith*."

Both twins looked at him, dumbstruck, and down at the man and his ring.

"Did she do this to him?" Taigan asked. "If she's the one—well,

45

we don't want to…" She swallowed and blew a breath out. "If this is her work, we should think about whether we want to find her."

"Not necessarily." He looked at the gaunt man. In Heffog, he had been attacked by people who killed for money or out of desperation. He fought them, but he hated it and wanted to target the people who pulled the strings, not those who put human shields between them and their enemies. His gaze settled on the twins. "What we should think about is what to *do* when we find her."

They looked wordlessly at him, afraid and uncomfortable.

And when he saw that, he came to a decision. They could not accompany him. He merely had to find a way to tell them—and get Prima to give them a new mission.

It was something to think about.

When he stood, he was surprised to see an unexpected figure waiting on the edge of the town square. "Orien," Ben said in surprise. "I didn't expect you to come yourself."

The elf came closer, his elegant features still and expressionless. He looked at the twins, who gazed at him, wide-eyed and confused, and stepped forward to crouch beside the body. Carefully, he studied the ring, the man's features, and the clothing.

Finally, he said a single word, too low for Ben to hear, and the ring vanished. In its wake, the man's hand blackened and curled as if it had been burned.

Orien stood, his face determinedly blank. "We should speak alone," he told Ben.

"Of course." He knew better than to think the twins would accept that, though. "First, let me introduce you to two travelers, Taigan and Jamie. They are on a mission of their own and helped me with this fight." A glare over Orien's head told the twins to stay quiet.

"I'm very pleased to meet you," the elf said to them politely.

"Take a meal with us," he suggested. "If you've come this far on your own, you have the time for it."

Orien nodded. Whatever he was about to say in response, however, it was lost in a storm of anguished chatter from the innkeeper's wife. She ran out the door, waving her hands at the scene in the town square.

His worry was that she knew the man they had killed. This turned out to not be the issue, however, and instead, she was incensed that Jamie had disregarded her order to rest for a week. She checked his bandage, wagged a finger at him, read him what was clearly the riot act in whatever language she spoke, and marched him into the inn by force.

"We should save him," Taigan said.

"Yeah, probably," Ben agreed.

Neither of them moved.

"Why...aren't you?" Orien asked them curiously.

"We're afraid she'll make *us* drink the tea if we go in there," the girl explained.

"There's nothing for it but to be brave, I suppose," the elf said finally. He sounded surprisingly cheerful. "Into battle, my friends. Our comrade is alone in the hands of the enemy." He set off, whistling.

"I like him," Taigan said, after a moment.

"So do I," he told her. Still, he couldn't help but remember Orien's eyes when he saw the ring—and the fact that he had come to deliver whatever the message was himself.

He had a feeling that things had become far more complicated.

CHAPTER SEVEN

I t was a while before Jamie managed to extricate himself from the ministrations of the innkeeper's wife, who constantly insisted that the wound would need to be recleaned. He had thought it would be easy enough to show her that he was healed, but she seemed to think he'd managed a trick of some kind and jabbed at his shoulder until he was fairly sure she would re-puncture it.

She muttered something he guessed was a ward against witchcraft and began to examine her various pots of salve, at which point he snuck out to join the others.

"I think she thinks I'm a witch," he said when he located them.

"And the tea?" Taigan asked.

"I didn't have any of that this time—no thanks to *you* lot, who didn't try to rescue me even once."

All three of them were suddenly focused on their beer and food.

"Traitors," the boy said darkly. "So—Orien, is it?"

"Yes." Orien nodded at him. "Taigan, yes?"

"Jamie, actually." He tried not to be prickly about that.

"Ah." The elf looked confused. "Human naming conventions

are very strange. Regardless, I am pleased to meet you both. What brings you to this town?"

The twins looked at each other. Jamie shrugged at his sister.

"Bad luck," she answered.

"A fine enough answer." Orien mopped some of the stew with his bread. "If bad luck troubles you, I wouldn't head north. Heffog is full of it these days. Or, rather, long-needed vengeance, which tends to catch people in the crossfire."

The boy considered this as the innkeeper brought him a bowl of stew. It hadn't been long since their breakfast, but it seemed that anytime they sat there, they were given food—and, as a perpetually hungry seventeen-year-old, he didn't complain.

"Perhaps we should go speak alone," Ben suggested to Orien.

"Nuh-uh," Taigan answered before the elf could. "You said you're looking for a goldsmith, there are weird gold rings on things that are attacking us, and we want to know what's going on."

Orien blinked at her and looked at Ben. "I see you told them who you were looking for."

"No specifics," he said. "Although I suppose the only specific I know about this woman is her name. I don't even know if she's human, elvish—"

"Half-elvish," the elf said. "Like me. You wouldn't know it— she looks full-human—but she has the magical talent of a full-blown elf."

"I didn't know humans and elves had different levels of talent," he said.

"Mmm." Orien took another mouthful and thought for a moment. "It's more the *way* they do magic. Elves can usually get the hang of it sooner or later and very few humans do, but if humans do, they tend to be quite powerful—like your friend Kural. And you, I'd guess."

"*Me?*" He looked flabbergasted.

The elf looked at the twins, both of whom shrugged in

response, and focused on Ben. "I thought you knew. You practically *spark* with magic. Didn't you know?" A wary look settled on his face and he rummaged in one of his pockets before he withdrew an iron ring. "Give me your hand. Yes. Wear this for now."

"Why?" Ben asked blankly. He looked at the twins, who both shrugged.

"Because you're a walking bomb," Orien told him sweetly. "And I'd rather not be anywhere close when your power first comes out."

"Uh…" He stared at his hand. "Huh."

"Anyway," the elf said with another sideways look at the iron ring, "Josyla had exceptional talent. If you want my opinion—and you really should—it's why she was so good at metalworking. Some of the best wizards in the world don't do magic for its own sake. They simply use it for their passion. Hers was gold."

"And that talent got her sold," Ben said softly.

"Yes. It's surprising, given how much Kerill could have made off her talent if he kept her. That's what made me think. I checked the records and…well, let's say her selling price was extraordinarily high and the money wasn't even half of it. He was playing the long game and had many of the other elves in thrall to him, magically speaking." He smiled grimly. "I'm glad the bastard's dead, and even more glad that I could do it."

Jamie didn't need to look at Taigan to know she was spooked. The twins looked at their food in utter silence.

"You're scaring them," Ben said.

"Good," Orien replied promptly. "Then maybe they won't go to Heffog."

He groaned and sounded genuinely exasperated, which Jamie liked. After their discussion, he was more ready to trust the other man—but he still felt he should keep his guard up.

"So…" The boy cleared his throat when everyone looked at him. He decided to be as neutral as he could about this. "It sounds like you found her trail."

"Yes." Orien gave him a tight smile and looked out into the town square. "She was bought by a sorceress, a woman who dabbled in very dark magic. Well. I say 'dabbled.' It was more than that. Kerill's records weren't very specific."

Ben frowned. "How did you find out, then?"

"I located one of his mistresses—who I happened to know was a great deal more intelligent than he gave her credit for—and explained what I needed to know. Between the two of us, we worked it out."

"How did you get the mistress to tell you?" Jamie asked, now suspicious. Taigan's look said she wondered the same thing.

"I asked," Orien said. He looked at the boy's expression. "I asked nicely so don't give me that look. She knew exactly who I was and what I had done, and she didn't have any particular love for him. Also, she knew why I was asking for the information." He shrugged. "It seems Kerill never told anyone much of anything except when he got angry. Then, he would threaten anyone in the vicinity with what he'd done to other people. Like, say, selling them to a sorceress who could control minds." He took a sip of his ale.

"And…" The girl paused, then soldiered on. "Are you worried that *she* might be controlled?"

The elf went silent for a long moment before he nodded.

Taigan looked at him. Almost gently, she asked, "How can we help?"

Orien gaped at her. He was about to respond when Ben interrupted.

"You two will stay out of this."

"The hell we will," she retorted.

"Yeah," Jamie added lamely.

"You will," he said flatly. "It's dangerous out here. That sorceress controlled the minds of however many people in Heffog, she's turning the poor into her personal army, and if you think for a *moment* that she'd let her prized goldsmith go without a fight, you're deluding yourselves. Orien and I will find a way to resolve this."

The silence that followed almost crackled with tension. Orien closed his mouth and sat, looking unnerved.

"No," Taigan said finally.

"No, *what*?" Ben glared at her.

"No, we won't simply let the two of you go off alone to rescue this woman," she said. "You're right, this sorceress won't let her go easily, which is why you need *help*."

"You're teenagers," he responded sharply. "Someone has to look out for you two, not lead you into danger."

"Yeah, well, I've been told that danger is the only thing that will make me better," she snapped. "That's why Prima led me into the fight with the bear-cat-thing, it's why… I…it's what I need." She seemed to have remembered that Orien didn't understand this.

Ben sighed. "I understand that," he said, "but I have seen some things in this world that I wouldn't wish on my worst enemy. I don't want to send you home traumatized."

"I'm confused," Orien said. "Are you ill?"

"In a way," Taigan said. She looked at him. "And I'm supposed to face danger here. It would make me stronger and it might cure me."

"There are many dangers," the elf said finally. "Perhaps you need dangers that are not quite so…well, dangerous."

"No." She didn't back down.

Jamie leaned back in his chair to watch. He couldn't keep from smirking. Neither Orien nor Ben had seen his sister's stubbornness, but they were in for a real surprise if they thought they would convince her to turn back.

"We will *not* discuss this around Orien," Ben said dangerously, "who has lost his fiancée and doesn't need her rescue to get turned into—"

"Ben." The elf put his hand on the other man's arm. "Think for a moment."

He sighed. "*What?*"

"You saw Heffog. You saw people beaten down, rudderless, and cowardly." Orien nodded his head in the direction of Jamie and Taigan. "These two want to help. They're brave. Shouldn't we encourage that?"

Frustrated, he muttered something and the elf leaned closer to say something in a low voice. When Ben started laughing, Jamie bristled, but he only nodded and looked at the twins.

"He's right," he said. "You two *would* go off and find a worse disaster if we didn't take you along."

"Now, wait a second—" the boy protested.

"Yes," Taigan said flatly, "we *would*."

"Taigan!"

"We're winning! Come on!"

Her brother put his head in his hands. "I hope to God that Mom and Dad don't hear about this or they'll kill me."

CHAPTER EIGHT

Unfortunately, even Orien did not know much. Over several mugs of ale, while Taigan and Jamie sparred out in the back, he shared the very few pieces of knowledge he had about the sorceress and his suspicions about Josyla.

It took an extraordinary amount of ale for him to admit them.

"The girl's question was good," he said finally. He held the mug as if for balance and stared blearily at the back wall. "That's why I came. Myself, I mean."

"Hmm?" Ben, who had been rather more restrained in his drinking, raised an eyebrow and tried not to laugh at the sight of the ever-elegant Orien swaying tipsily.

"The girl." He tried to jerk his head at the yard and swayed drunkenly but managed to steady himself with visible effort. "This ale...strong."

"You've also had about twelve mugs of it," he pointed out.

"*Have* I?" the elf tipped his mug and looked intently at the bottom of it as if that might hold the answer. "Huh. It's good. Anyway. The girl was right—about what you'll find when you find Josyla."

"You think she's mind-controlled?" Ben, who could have

dumped his beer on Taigan's head when she brought it up, wasn't surprised but he hadn't wanted to be right about this.

"Yes and no." Orien's fingers had tightened around the mug. "It's…I think she might be working for her willingly."

"*What?*" That, he had *not* expected.

"Yeah." His companion looked at him with a frown. "And she wasn't my fiancée, you know. Only a friend." The mournful way he said it showed that he, at least, had wanted it to be more.

Ben made a noncommittal noise while he took a sip of his beer.

"She…" Orien sighed.

"You loved her," he said and cut to the chase. "She had good qualities."

"Yes. She wasn't a monster or anything." The elf looked miserable. "Only…resentful. Resentful of us being servants for being bastard-born while our half-siblings were lords and ladies. Resentful that so many in the city didn't have food. All of it. It wasn't that she was mean. She merely saw so much cruelty and felt powerless because she would never be rich enough to help. After a while, she even looked down on herself for being a goldsmith."

"Why?"

"Because it only helped our lord," Orien said. "She loved her work but she said she didn't want to enrich him."

"Shouldn't she feel the same way about the sorceress, then?"

"Maybe." He looked doubtful. "The thing is…look, I couldn't tell you why I'm so sure of this, but when I heard who had bought her—that it was a sorceress who used black magic—all I could think was that Josyla had decided to learn from her. She was clever and she'd learn all kinds of things you never expected her to from the details she needed to put into a certain piece of jewelry or an offhand comment. I'd bet she learned magic, whether the sorceress meant to teach her or not."

Ben sighed.

"I'm only saying," Orien said, "that you need to be careful. And...think about whether you want to do this."

He looked at him. "If I don't, though, you'll always wonder."

The elf looked away.

"And maybe you'll try to find her yourself," he continued quietly.

Orien said nothing.

"And you might have to make a choice you don't want to make," he continued, "about how to deal with her."

Although he said nothing, his elvish features were twisted with pain.

"I'll go," Ben said, "and if she was tricked or coerced or anything like that, I'll bring her home. If there's any way, I'll do it."

"Thank you," Orien said quietly. He stood drunkenly. "I should get back. They need me. This was the worst time to go but I couldn't tell a messenger what I told you. You should start with a woman named Yulia. She and the sorceress worked together."

He held his tongue and simply nodded as he saw Orien to the door and watched him set out. From the speed with which the elf faded into the distance, he suspected that he had a travel spell of some kind on him.

Being that drunk, he'd better be careful or he'd wind up miles off course. He smiled at the thought and returned to his drink.

Once he'd drained his tankard, he left word with the innkeeper that he was going to see Yulia. The man seemed bemused that he would visit an old woman, but there was no hint of scandal in the way he nodded. Whatever she had done with the sorceress, she didn't seem to be known as one.

Ben snuck out, hoped the twins would take time with their sparring—after all, the energy of a teenager could go almost indefinitely—and headed down the country road, whistling quietly. Despite his misgivings, or perhaps because of them, he concentrated on how beautiful the day was. The night's rain had turned the grass and trees a brilliant green, while the blue sky and warm sun set everything off perfectly.

Yulia lived a mile or so away from the cluster of buildings that comprised the heart of the town. It was farther than he would have thought an old woman would live but then again, it sounded like she was not merely a helpless old woman.

She was working in the garden when he arrived. Herbs and vegetables were planted in neat rows without a weed in sight. A stone wall covered in lichen and moss surrounded the yard, with a flowering apple tree on one side of the gate and a pretty, thatched cottage in the center of it with smoke rising from its chimney.

The old woman stood as he came close and hobbled forward to open the gate.

"Did you know I was coming?" he asked her, confused.

"Of course. Your thoughts were loud enough for a half-addled cow to hear them." She gave him a piercing look from under bushy brows and waved him in. "Come on, then. The tea should be steeped."

"Er…thank you." He followed her along the path and into the house.

It was tiny. A little bed was covered with a patchwork quilt, a rocker at the hearth held a basket with yarn and knitting needles, and the other side of the room was taken up with a long wooden workbench covered with stacks of cloth, spools of thread, and a few jars of spices. A teapot sat on a ceramic tile with two mugs next to it.

Yulia waved him to the bed to sit while she poured them tea. She hobbled back, sat in the rocking chair, and then said baldly,

"So, it's the goldsmith Gwyna bought, eh?"

"Do we need to have a conversation?" Ben asked. "Or have you read all my thoughts already?"

"Don't be smart with me, young man." She moved fretfully and her gnarled fingers closed and shifted around the warmth of the mug. "Your thoughts came through muddled—oh, clear enough for me to guess who you wanted to find, but little else. Gold, I saw, and a terrible beast. An elvish woman. But, *you*...who are you?"

"No one important."

"That's not true in the slightest," she said at once. "You killed an emissary of the new elvish king, boy. I'd not say you're unimportant."

He leaned back in his chair. "How did you know that?"

"You dreamed of it last night."

"I..." He had, and the thought that someone could hear his dreams was deeply unpleasant.

"It takes an unusual talent to hear thoughts," she told him. "And they've been less clear since *this* was put on you." She extended her hand to tap the iron ring. "Which brings me to your problem. You need to find Gwyna and you need to do it without her realizing who you are and why you're there."

Ben waited.

Yulia sighed. "She was a quiet one, Gwyna. Always quiet. She kept her thoughts hidden and worked hard. I never saw the darkness in her. There are some you know will go bad, but she wasn't one. She was mild-mannered and nothing special to look at, with no great talent for fire or ice or any of the things that level towns. In most cases, their parents would come to me begging for help. She arrived on her own."

He took a sip of his tea. It was surprisingly light, both fruity and bitter, and oddly refreshing despite its temperature.

"But she always drew the dark ones," the woman told him. "Angry ones and bitter ones. And now, she's far away and her name is never spoken, and that worries me all the more."

"You think someone needs to deal with her," he said.

"You say it very simply," she observed. "You're a strange one, aren't you? Hating violence and craving justice. A word to the wise, child—justice comes slowly and it hits wide. It'll cost more than you want every time and give you less than you hoped. If you took my advice, I'd say to avoid Gwyna and her goldsmith. But, since you won't..."

Ben chuckled and took another sip.

Yulia smiled. The smile showed him, only for a moment, how she must have been as a young woman. What was in her past, he wondered? She was a magic user, an old woman without regrets and with no hint of family or loss, and yet there must be loss to give her such wit and warnings.

"You should ask for Gwyna's help," the woman said. She tapped the ring. "Ask her to train you. She'll take you."

"Why?"

"She doesn't want justice," she told him, "and doesn't care one whit about it. But the desperation for it makes people angry and she's always been good at harnessing that anger. If she thinks she can use you, she'll take you in."

"But getting in is only part of it," Ben protested. "What if she's bound the goldsmith's mind? How am I supposed to get her out? And what if I have to kill her? How do I kill a sorceress so powerful she can enslave minds and still no one knows about her?"

Yulia gave him a sardonic look. "That isn't the world's problem to solve, is it? It's yours, boy. So find the answers. If you want justice, you had better be prepared to mete it out."

He stiffened a little and swallowed. "And where is she?"

"There's a warren of caves to the south on the shores of the lake. They are difficult to get to but not impossible."

He nodded and thought for a moment but jumped when someone pounded on the door.

"That'll be the two," the woman said.

"The two what?" Ben asked. Immediately, though, he realized he should have known the answer. The door opened and Taigan stuck her head around it.

"There you are," she said accusingly. "You tried to leave us behind." Then, to the woman, she added, "I'm sorry. I'm Taigan."

"Aye, and a strange one, you are." Yulia looked appraisingly at her. "Well, come in, both of you. We should decide what to do with the two of you while yon wizard goes off to free the goldsmith."

"We're going with him," the girl said at once.

"That, you most certainly are *not*. No, don't you argue with me, young lady." The old woman gave her a hard look. "We'll find something for you two here."

"But I need to help someone," Taigan said. "I can't sit around thinking and trying to shift myself between worlds anymore. I *can't*. I need to be in danger and I need to help someone. It's the only way I'll get better. I want to go home."

Yulia, who could not have understood any of the context behind that statement, watched the girl contemplatively. Ben thought she seemed to be looking beyond the specifics to see the shape of the truth despite not understanding anything about comas and pods.

"You've met some of her creatures," she said. "Gwyna's. They escaped her but her bindings still hold. I could teach you to free them and bring them back to the human world."

The twins looked at each other and now, he was the one who felt uncertain.

"They shouldn't be alone," he said cautiously.

"They won't be," she said simply. "They have each other, don't they? The problem with you, young man, is that you try to do everything at once and run off when it doesn't work. Set your sights on one goal and go from there."

Ben sighed.

"I'll take care of these two," the woman told him. "You go and find Gwyna. Do what must be done. I'll help these two."

"What? *Now*?" This all seemed far too sudden.

"Yes." Yulia stood and began to shoo him out the door. "Don't waste any time. You'll only talk yourself out of it."

"But—uh—" He reached the door and looked over her head at the twins. "Are you okay with this?"

"I…think so?" Taigan shrugged.

"They'll run off if they aren't," the old woman said practically. "Along with you, young man."

The door slammed in his face and he gaped at it.

"She has a point about you trying to do too much at once," Prima said.

"Oh, not you too."

"I'm just saying…"

He rolled his eyes and started south. "Where is this lake? Could I reach it by nightfall?"

"Actually, the team wanted to pull you out for some physical therapy. I'll deposit you at the lake when you come into the game again."

"Oh." He looked around. "Should I find somewhere to lie down or—"

The world dissolved into blue.

"I guess that answers that question."

CHAPTER NINE

When Ben opened his eyes, the feeding tube had already been withdrawn and the monitors had been unclipped from his fingers and chest. He struggled to sit and rejected an offered hand, although he couldn't see whose it was.

"Let me try," he rasped, hoarse from the feeding tube.

"Sure." The hand withdrew and the person watched him.

When he managed to get up after a very undignified struggle, Nick smiled at him.

"You know, I won't say our pod hasn't done *anything* for you but I have to say, I think most of your progress is due to you being a stubborn bastard." He cleared his throat. "No offense meant."

"None taken." He coughed and winced. "I don't like feeding tubes."

"Yeah. I'll see if we can arrange to put you under for only twelve hours at a time or so," the engineer said. "Normally, someone in a comatose state could wait much longer, but the virtual reality keeps your metabolism going and—whoa, hey!"

Ben had tried to push himself off the edge of the pod and

almost faceplanted into the floor. Nick barely caught him and grunted with the effort.

"Jesus Christ, are you made of solid muscle?"

"I used to be," he said bitterly.

"Uh-huh. Well, either you still are, or your bones are made of titanium." The man pivoted and tried to hold him up. "Almost... okay, can you stand?"

"Yeah. Wait...dizzy." He went backward, and—to his immense surprise—landed in a chair. "Huh?"

"We saw that Nick was having trouble," Jacob said. He came around to look at him. "Also, for the record, you're not wearing any underwear, so maybe less running around in a hospital gown."

"Oh, fuck." He went bright red.

Nick snickered. "Okay, mister, you know the drill—coordination tests and hydration, then you can have food."

"Underwear first," Ben said.

"I...won't argue with that." Nick stared at him with his arms folded. "How to get you into an exam room, though? You're not in a wheelchair."

"I have an idea." DuBois pushed a low cart on wheels beside him. "Put him on this."

"Sure," Jacob said. "That's not abandoning our duty of care at *all*."

"I am your patient," he said, "and I am telling you to not show my butt to any more people!"

"I don't think that provides legal coverage," Jacob responded. "So don't sue us if you fall off this."

"Uh-huh." He tried to steady himself as the team lifted his chair onto the cart and set off. "Ohhhh, I think I'm going to be sick."

"No throwing up on the ride, please," Nick said, "and keep your hands and feet inside the cart area at all times."

"Okay, but why are you *videotaping* this?"

"For our records," Jacob said without any shred of remorse. "Don't worry, we won't show them to Eliza."

"You'd better fucking not," he muttered.

He desperately hoped they didn't show Eliza what happened in the next few minutes. From wiggling his toes to walking in various lines, he was asked to do a number of very simple tasks, most of which he could not do at all gracefully.

"This sucks," Ben said flatly.

"Okay, remember that all the doctors are calling us and saying we're liars," Jacob said. "You're doing the eighteen-month exercises for this and it's only been what...three? Three months, I think."

"People go on like this for eighteen months?" he asked, horrified. "That's how long everyone thought it would take?"

The two younger men were suddenly very busy with paperwork, but DuBois answered promptly,

"Yes, and *also*—" He broke off with a yelp when his bag of popcorn tipped off the table and scattered.

"Oops," Nick said. He met Ben's gaze with the most limpid, innocent expression he could imagine. "Time for more tests and then you can have pizza."

He wanted to protest but his stomach wanted pizza so he gave in with a grumble.

The next few hours passed with too-small meals and far too many coordination and strength exercises. He was given a set of weights so small they barely deserved the name and had to begin weight training with two of the physical trainers.

Both were relentless. Ben, who had thought he was a prime example of stubbornness, had nothing on either of the two. No matter how red his face got or how his muscles started to shake, they guided him through the exercises and the allotted number of repetitions and made notes calmly.

By the end of it, he was covered in sweat, aching, and absolutely ravenous. He barely made it to the table for dinner and could have cried with happiness to see a giant bowl of pad thai and a second of red curry.

It hurt to raise each bite to his mouth, but it was worth it.

"So," Jacob said, as Ben shoveled food in, "how are Taigan and Jamie doing?"

He paused. The other man's tone was slightly too casual.

"Is something wrong?" he asked.

The engineer's expression flickered.

"I'm not good at all that subtle 'avoiding topics' stuff," he said. "So…is something wrong?"

Jacob sighed. "I can't tell you most of it. I only wanted your impression of the two of them."

"They're nice," he said. "Teenagers. I don't know what you want me to say." He suddenly looked over his shoulder. "Wait, they're out there, aren't they? In the lab? That's as trippy as fuck."

"I also can't tell you about where they are," the other man said. "Anyway, it looked like Jamie wasn't too sure of you, but that seems to have calmed."

"It was mostly understandable," Ben said through a mouthful of noodles. "We've all seen dudes be skeevy. But Taigan doesn't take shit from anyone. He doesn't need to worry."

"What's she like?" Jacob was curious now. "We've never…met her. Only seen her in the game sometimes."

"Oh, right. The coma. Um…I don't think she likes to let people in." He scratched his scalp and considered. "She told me about the coma and how she wanted to help someone to get better, but I don't think she told me anything about *her*."

"It's a family full of strong personalities," his companion said wryly. "If you think Taigan takes no shit, you should meet their older sister. Honestly, you can probably be glad you didn't. She wouldn't have sat you down to talk to you like Jamie did and would have merely stabbed you."

"They're protective of her," he observed. "She's the baby of the family and she keeps getting sick. I suppose it makes it sense."

"Yeah." Jacob took a sip of iced tea. "Keep eating. After this, you'll need to fast for ten hours."

"Ugh." He began to wolf his food again. "I do *not* like that."

"You don't say. Anyway, Taigan was...there wasn't anything *off?*"

"I don't know how you mean," he had to admit. "She's a strong personality, but that's not unusual in a teenager—especially one who's going through this. Seriously, though, why?"

"I can't say. I really can't." Jacob shook his head. "But thank you. Hearing from someone who's been in there and interacted with her is very reassuring."

Ben knew he wouldn't get any further if he pried. For all their joking, the PIVOT team took privacy very seriously.

"One thing, though," he said. "Is there anything I should watch out for? Anything you want me to draw attention to immediately?"

The young engineer considered this very seriously. "Not that I can think of," he said finally. "But thank you for asking."

"Sure." He scooped up the last mouthful of noodles. "Okay, I'm ready to stop eating for now. I'll have regrets in a few hours, though."

"On the plus side, you're doing very well so you won't have to do this too many more times." Jacob smiled and came to offer a hand to pull him up. "How are things looking for when you're out on your own again?"

"Ugh, don't say that." He grimaced. "Your CEO is trying to get me a job in military stuff and...I don't know."

"You don't have to take it, you know," Jacob assured him. "She comes across a little scary, but she genuinely wants to help people."

"I only, uh..." Ben shrugged. "I wanted to change the world, you know?"

"I do know," the other man said honestly. "About six months ago, I found that I'd done the best work of my life for an eight hundred dollars a day machine no one could afford. It was 'only a videogame' and wouldn't help anyone. And, a few days after that, I realized how it could help people."

"So what's your take on that life lesson?" Ben asked. "Steer into the skid?"

Jacob laughed ruefully. "I wish I had a good life lesson to take from that. I think the only one is, don't fold. Because we had no idea where that would go."

"Good point." They had reached his makeshift little bedroom and he opened the door to smile at the bed. A real bed sounded nice right about now. After so much food and a day of exertion, he was ready to pass out.

After one more thing. He said goodnight to Jacob and headed to the computer to bring his email up.

He read through the stories of his friends' exploits with a smile. Locked away in a virtual world, he had asked if they would send him updates each day about the mundane little things to remind him what the real world was like. There were stories about printer cartridges, expired coconut milk, and new puppies.

Mike and Natasha's honeymoon had been wonderful and they had sent him pictures of them eating ice cream and leaning against trees, as well as going to a baseball game and buying ridiculous tourist apparel. He even saw a few shots of himself as their officiant, something that made him smile.

Eliza's email was the last one he opened. He hadn't wanted to ask her to email him every day and he was glad to see that she'd stuffed her message full of things they had talked about on their first date. She included a podcast recommendation and a link to a study she had cited, with an apologetic note that she had misstated the effects by two percent—something he could not imagine anyone other than her apologizing for.

He replied with notes about his physical therapy and took care to include all the terms he hadn't understood. Not only could she clarify, but she and the other doctors at the Aspen hospital were also tracking his progress with great interest. Remembering how much of an ass he'd been right after the accident, he was trying to make it up to them with updates.

At last, he eased into bed and stretched. It was strange how divorced he felt, both from reality and from the game. Ben could see the choices stretching out before him and how easy it would be tomorrow to fall into the world of the game without another thought, putting his safety on the line for Orien or the twins.

At the same time, he could see how his time there was coming to an end. He would miss it, he thought, but the purpose of the game for him hadn't been to provide a place where he would thrive and enjoy himself. It had been to force him to confront all the parts of himself he tried to avoid.

As his thoughts drifted, he wondered how much of that had been a set-up and how much of it had been what he went looking for. He was willing to bet that most of it was the latter. The team, after all, hadn't known much about him.

That was interesting. He'd gone looking for the very things he always ran away from in real life.

He wanted to turn that over in his head, but the day had caught up with him. A little clumsily, he managed to roll over on the bed but didn't even have the covers up when he fell asleep.

CHAPTER TEN

Ben had barely walked out the door when Yulia pointed at the little bed and said, "*Sit*, both of you."

The twins exchanged a look.

"Was that too complicated an instruction?" she asked acerbically.

"No," Taigan said.

"But it's not very friendly," Jamie added. "You won't turn us into frogs, will you?"

"Why on *earth* would I turn you into a frog?" She planted her hands on her hips. "What purpose could that possibly serve?"

Neither twin answered and both looked at the floor. Taigan hoped she wouldn't make her answer for Jamie's question, and she had the sense that he—the little weasel—hoped *he* wouldn't be made to reply.

"Well?" Yulia demanded.

Taigan elbowed her brother.

"Ow! I, uh—it's what witches do. In stories." He blushed such a bright red that it was a wonder he didn't burst into flames then and there.

The old woman snorted. "Well, that's not true. Young man, I

have no intention of turning anyone into anything. I simply intend to tell two headstrong and not overly wise children about the dangers of the forest. *Sit*."

Both twins sat. The bed was made for Yulia's diminutive height and was therefore low enough that their knees stuck up awkwardly. That fact was not improved when she handed them earthenware cups of tea. Taigan balanced hers on one of her knees and wrapped her fingers around it.

"So you've seen Gwyna's beasts, then?" she said when she sat in her rocking chair.

"Yes…ma'am." The girl hunched her shoulders. "Twice."

"Tell me about the encounters," she said and listened while Taigan and Jamie told the story together, often prompting one another with details.

When they finished, the woman tipped her head back and gazed into the fireplace. She suddenly looked surprisingly old and was troubled by what she had heard. That much had been clear from her wary looks as the two spoke.

"The elf man," she said finally. "You said he spoke a single word and the ring crumbled to dust?"

The young people both nodded.

"What was that spell?" Taigan asked.

"It wasn't…hmm." Yulia frowned in thought. "Do you remember how in old, old legends, you're never to tell a fae creature your name? There's a power in names, and some things hate hearing their own. Dark magic is one of those—a dark magic spell twists something away from its nature. Being reminded of what it is while it is so perverted causes its destruction." She tapped her mouth. "I'd pay good money to know which word he said—if he named it gold or a ring…but no matter."

"So if you know something's name while it's transformed, you can destroy it?" Jamie asked. "Would that work with the animals?"

"An excellent question, young man, and the answer is that yes, it very well might—*if* you knew the best name to call it. For a living being, that's tricky. It's safer by far to train with the sword." She looked sternly at them. "Either way, it seems Gwyna is up to something dark and I'll not have that in my home. While your friend goes to cut things off at the source, you two can help me protect the village."

Jamie looked at Taigan. *Do we trust her?*

She replied with a tiny nod.

"How do we help you?" the girl asked.

"There are two places of power in the forest nearby," Yulia said, "a wellspring and a maze. Go to both and find out if anyone has conducted rituals there. What you're looking for are candles or lanterns—or candle wax, lamp oil, any of that—the remains of diagrams in charcoal or chalk, the remains of a sacrifice, or anything in gold or silver. Both of those conduct magic, while iron stops it."

Taigan bit her lip. "Um…where in the forest?"

"That's your first test, isn't it?" the woman asked lightly. "Prove to me you can find those places *and* find your way back safely, then I can entrust you with larger tasks."

The twins nodded to one another and stood. She drained her tea hastily and her brother inspected his, sniffed, and drank it with a look of relief.

"Now, there's the look of someone who's had Korilla's tea lately," Yulia said with a chuckle. "Were you injured, boy?"

"Yes. Korilla is the innkeeper's wife?"

"Yes. Raised in the steppes. I don't think she speaks a word of common to this day, but I don't need to know her words to know she's a good soul. She heals anyone who comes to her—there's an old magic in those potions, I think."

"You *think*?" he asked. "I had a three-inch puncture wound from that monster and it was gone in a few hours. Of course, she *did* look surprised…"

A strange look settled on Yulia's face. "How strange," she

mused. "The odds are, she's not gotten better at magic without realizing it, at least not so late in her life. So that would suggest it's the herbs...or in the air. The water, mayhap?" She shook her head and stood. "You two go and find the wellspring and the maze. I have plenty to search for here while you're gone."

With surprising speed, they were hustled outside and stood in the sunlight, gaping at one another and their surroundings.

"Prima," Jamie said finally, "do you think *you* can help us?"

"You can at least determine where the forest is, right?"

"That part we got, thank you," he said, his tone prickly. Indeed, the forest took up half the horizon, green and sunlit from there, and perhaps a quarter of a mile behind Yulia's house.

Taigan snorted. "He's right, though," she told Prima. "It's a very big forest."

"Yes, but remember what she said. Showing that you can navigate the forest and keep yourselves safe shows that you have the skill to be given more challenging assignments."

"Okay, but *you* remember that if we—"

Taigan touched Jamie's arm as they set off for their destination. "She's made her decision," she said. "And what's the worst that happens?"

"We *die.*"

"Don't be dramatic. We wander around lost for a little while and the team pulls us out of the simulation. In all likelihood? We wander around for a little while, get lost, find a way out, and don't find anything useful." She shrugged. "And I think the best way to do this is to not get lost in the first place."

The twins bickered good-naturedly about markings and counting measures as they walked to the forest, and by the time they reached it, they had come up with a series of symbols to mark their route. They had decided to mark trees with the choice they made—turning in one direction, going straight, or doubling back. They would mark both their angle of approach and the way they had left.

Soon enough, they passed from the sunlight into the dappled shade of the forest's edge. Younger trees stood with more space between them, leaves rustled under their feet, and birds called from somewhere beyond. Taigan was glad to see that even in the deepest parts of the forest, there was still a good deal of light.

"I hope the trees in here aren't alive," she said as she carved some symbols into one of them.

"You know how trees work, right?"

She rolled her eyes at the sky while Jamie snickered. "Yes, thank you. I only meant if they were sentient or something. I don't want to piss them off."

The twins ventured through dips that contained ice-cold streams and over hillocks that left their palms dirty and their lungs burning. On more than one occasion, one of them tumbled and stifled a yelp. They kept their noise to a minimum, however, not wanting to draw the attention of whatever might be lurking there.

Thankfully, Taigan tripped over the first marker or they would have missed it. She hissed in through her teeth and hopped on her other foot, clutching her wounded toes. When Jamie looked back, she pointed and let him inspect while she eased her foot out of her boot to inspect it.

"It's old," he said finally in a low tone. "And covered in lichen and all that. Come look at it."

She muttered as she stooped to see. The marker was covered with runes, although they were difficult to read under the lichen. No two sides of the four-sided stone seemed to be the same.

Finally, she shrugged. They had no idea how to read it. All they could do was look for more of them.

"Ah-hem."

"What?" they whispered in unison.

"I can translate things."

"I thought you weren't helping," Taigan replied waspishly.

"I can translate things."

"Okay, what does it say?" Jamie asked.

"On the side Taigan stubbed her toe on, it says 'Ahead, lies protection.' Moving clockwise, the other sides read first, "Seek the haven," next, "For that alone is yours," and finally, "Greed will doom you."

"Huh." The girl folded her arms. "So it wants us to continue this way for protection…"

"But not look for anything else," Jamie finished. "Do you think it's the maze?"

They set off again.

"How would you seek shelter in a maze?" His sister asked reasonably. "It must be something else ahead because—ow! Son of a bitch!"

"Hey, another one," he said brightly. "You have a talent for this."

"It was the same toe." She moaned and whimpered slightly. "Okay, Prima, what does this godforsaken hunk of rock say?"

"The same things," the AI said promptly.

"Right." Taigan set off again once she'd snatched a stick up to thrust ahead of her in the undergrowth. This tactic caught the next stone before she tripped over it. "Ha!"

"So, we've thrown caution to the winds, I see." Jamie looked up. "Prima, is this one the same?"

"This one has no markings."

"Curiouser and curiouser," he said. He pushed through the undergrowth nearby and caught his breath. "Taigan, be careful."

She moved cautiously to his side and saw immediately what he had meant. They stood at the top of the wall that surrounded the maze. Four feet down, the maze itself was lined with stone walls that used no mortar and yet seemed entirely untouched by time. There were no weeds or uneven ground.

The entire location seemed to exist in a bubble.

"Protection," Taigan said softly. "Do we dare go in, do you think? What if we can't get out?"

"I think it'll be fine as long as we don't look for more," Jamie said. "They must mean searching for artifacts or something, right?"

"But we're looking for information," she said. "What if we lift something up or move it and a trap comes down?"

They looked at each other, then at the sky.

"*I have no idea,*" Prima said, absolutely unconvincing in her innocence.

"Of course, you don't," the girl muttered. "Well, we were sent to find the maze and we're here. I'd say that Yulia would have warned us if we couldn't get out, but maybe that was part of the test. Let's walk along the edge and see what we can see inside, then go in if we don't see anything worrying."

"Good call." He nodded.

They walked carefully around the edge, careful to never let their arms swing into the air above the maze. It was a strange kind of protection, Taigan thought, without any roof or high walls, and yet, it seemed frozen in time without even leaves on the ground.

Which made the sacrifice all the more apparent once they saw it. She clapped a hand over her mouth and stopped dead.

From where she stood to the center of the maze was one long line. If you didn't follow the pattern of steps, you could have stepped easily over the tiny stone wall as the layer around the center was only a couple of inches tall.

Taigan didn't think they should do that. Although she couldn't say why, she was utterly *sure* that she should follow the path.

She was also sure that several dead animals lay inside separate diagrams at the center of the maze.

"This is what we were looking for, wasn't it?" She looked at Jamie. "Come on. Stick to the path and *don't* pick anything up."

CHAPTER ELEVEN

Taigan had feared the smell of the bodies, but whatever kept things from being touched by time or lichen or rain in this area had also stopped the sacrifices from decaying. The three bodies lay still and the tiny amounts of blood they saw had not dried. There were no flies or maggots.

Somehow, that was more unsettling.

Worse—as they saw each time the path brought them close—was the fact that the three bodies were of young animals. She had her suspicions of what they would see, but when at last they came into the heart of the maze and she could be certain, she wanted to cry.

"A wolf cub," she said quietly.

"And a kitten—a bobcat, maybe?" Jamie asked. "And…"

She stared at the pile of fur, her expression almost a mask that showed no emotion. "I think it's a bear," she said finally. Her voice was thin and high. "The things we saw—the monsters—we couldn't tell if they were cats, wolves, or bears. I think they're all three."

"This was where she made the spell," he whispered in reply. "And it won't decay…"

The twins looked at one another.

"We shouldn't touch anything," Taigan said, but there was no certainty in her.

"This is wrong," he said fiercely. "They deserve a burial."

"What if we make it worse? What if we don't undo the spell?" She stared at them and fumbled to clutch his hand. "I want to destroy all of this, but what if I simply make it worse?"

Her brother looked around. "We have to assume this was all deliberate," he said finally. "Whoever did this—probably Gwyna —chose a place where the diagrams would be untouched and the bodies wouldn't be disturbed. The diagrams are here, which means they're important, so we should destroy those. Look here."

He took her hand and led her to one side of a diagram. The symbol there had been dug a little deeper than the rest of it and something seemed to glitter beneath it—energy, disturbed and raw like an open wound.

"Okay," Taigan said. She nodded. "We need to bring the bodies out and dig them graves, and also destroy the diagrams."

"Diagrams first," Jamie said. He drew his sword and looked up. "Uh...if anything is watching, we're not trying to take anything that belongs to the maze. We're trying to heal it."

He placed the tip of the sword at the outer edge of one diagram and drew a line through it to the center. At first, it seemed remarkably anticlimactic.

A second later, a blast of energy hurled him off his feet.

"Jamie!"

"Ow," he protested and followed it with a startled yelp. The little wolf cub had scrambled to its feet and now snapped and growled at him.

Taigan hauled him up and out of the way. She knelt and stretched her hands out. "We're not going to hurt you," she said.

The little wolf stared at them. Blood trickled down its fur now. It backed away warily, and when they did not follow, it turned and raced into the maze.

"They're alive," she whispered. "Quick, give me the sword."

"Maybe only one of us should have concussions," her brother suggested. He stood and put out the sword again. "Although maybe give me something to wrap around my head."

She wound her cloak around his head like a turban, giggled, and stood nearby with her arms out as he drew a line across the second diagram. Again, energy released itself in a blast and he slammed back into her arms, but the two of them together managed to stay standing.

"Only one more," she said encouragingly.

"Yep." Jamie shook his head to clear it. "Are your ears ringing? Mine are. Okay, get behind me again. Three, two...ow, fuck."

Taigan snickered into his turban. She levered him to the ground and looked at the little animals that hauled themselves up. The tiny bobcat chirped piteously, then hissed, and the bear growled low in its throat. Like the wolf, they both ran from the humans.

That was probably a fair instinct, she had to admit.

When they were gone, she knelt and hesitated. She didn't want to put her bare skin on the spell but somehow, the thought seemed right. Cautiously, she started with the edges and brushed the dirt smooth and back into place. She took care to erase only one line at a time, and it wasn't long before the first diagram was completely gone.

To her shock, the ground looked as if it had never been touched at all.

Heartened, she repeated the process. The area seemed healed and a spark of energy against her palm startled her but wasn't unpleasant.

"Hey," Jamie said, surprised, "my head feels better."

Taigan stood and brushed her pants off. She nodded and looked around worriedly. "I think we should go. She might come back to see why the spell was lost."

"Right." He moved to step over the little wall.

"The *right* way, you heathen."

They hurried out of the maze and glanced around at every opportunity to see if anyone was watching. No one seemed to be. There were a couple of drops of blood where the animals must have run, but the fact that there was only one way through the maze seemed to have led all three of the sacrifices out.

"Imagine how evil you'd have to be to use animals that way," Taigan said fiercely. "Little animals—babies—and she kept them alive and in pain this whole time, suspended between life and death."

Jamie looked soberly at her. "And Ben is walking into that. I'm worried about him. Prima, can you warn him?"

"That is kind of you," Prima said after a pause. *"I attempt to not give players information they have not seen with their own eyes, but...I will consider it."*

"I think that's the best we'll get out of her," he told his sister. "Do think about it, Prima. He needs to understand that this is...a little different than we thought. It's not merely hurting people. It's worse."

"Do humans honestly think of hurting animals as worse than hurting humans?"

"It's complicated," Taigan said. "But torturing baby animals? Yeah, that's bad."

"I see."

Privately, the girl wondered if Prima had accidentally created a villain who was much more villainous than she had intended, but she didn't ask. The AI tended to be very self-conscious about instances of messing up.

They had barely stepped into the forest when they heard a crashing noise and the whimpering sounds of someone in great pain. Both twins froze, and when she wanted to dash forward, her brother clamped a hand around her wrist. He held a finger up to his lips and the two of them found hiding places behind trees.

It wasn't long before the source of the noise became clear—a human, gaunt and delirious, stumbled through the woods in ragged clothing.

"No, no, no..." He moaned. There was blood on his teeth.

And a gold ring on his finger.

Jamie and Taigan looked at one another and he gestured emphatically for her to stay in hiding. The man stumbled on, oblivious and paranoid by turns. He seemed confused and yet to have some awareness of where he was.

When he was gone, she crept out and motioned for her brother to follow.

"What are you doing?" he mouthed at her.

She held a finger to her lips and gestured for him to follow. He scowled but couldn't stop her without making a scene so simply complied.

The man thrust through briars and tripped over downed trees. He pushed himself to his feet each time he fell and continued. His strength seemed, however, like the fevered thrashings of a seriously ill patient overlying a deep weariness that might claim him at any moment.

Taigan's hatred for Gwyna grew with every step. Torturing young animals, taking the poor and sick for her experiments... she needed to be stopped. She was furious now that Yulia hadn't let them go with Ben. While she had never particularly liked the feeling of killing their various adversaries—beyond the fact that she didn't want to die and was being attacked—she was very sure she would enjoy killing the sorceress.

That thought scared her so much that she stopped dead in her tracks and Jamie ran into her with a muffled exclamation. They crouched in the undergrowth in case the man had heard them.

"Are you okay?" Her brother's voice was barely audible.

"Yes, I...yes." She shook her head. "Later."

She had been faced with any number of choices over the years and those had been painful, but all of them had dealt with what she wanted if something happened to her medically. She had never, even in her wildest dreams, imagined being faced with a choice like this.

It had simply never occurred to her to wonder if a side of her might enjoy killing someone. It wasn't merely unpleasant or unwelcome, it was an utter shock.

When they caught up with the man, he had come to a camp of sorts. In reality, it could hardly be called that and at first glance, it was horrifying. Bones and blood were everywhere, the bones twisted and shattered, and the people among them had blood on their mouths.

But they had been wolves when this happened, she realized. She and Jamie had undone the spell, stripping away the qualities of each animal when they freed the sacrifices, and the spell that had turned these people into monsters had disintegrated.

Now they were human, and they were weak and still in pain.

She wanted to help them, but this time, it was cowardice that held her back. These people still wore Gwyna's rings and the gold bit into the flesh. Even if they were no longer monsters, who could say if they would attack others on sight?

Taigan backed away quietly and motioned for Jamie to do so as well. They crept away into the forest and followed the trail of broken branches and their signs out of the forest. By mutual and silent agreement, they did not seek out the wellspring yet.

They had learned enough already that Yulia should know about.

They were close to the edge of the forest when her brother said, his voice subdued, "What do you think that maze was?"

She looked at him in surprise. "How do you mean?"

"Well, they said protection could be anyone's if they wanted it, but not to look for anything else," he said. "That's interesting. Was there a trapdoor into a tomb full of artifacts, Indiana Jones-style, or was it only the magic they didn't want people to touch? If so, why didn't Gwyna bite it?" His tone softened. "I think it's nice that…it's, like, they built it for something else but they also made it a haven for anyone."

"I hadn't thought of that," she responded thoughtfully. "I suppose it's the only place where those animals would have survived. She found a way to turn that into something dark, but…" She shook her head. "Back there, what scared me was that I thought I'd enjoy killing her. I don't like thinking like that."

He looked at her and moved closer to wrap an arm around her shoulders. The noonday sunlight was bright outside the forest, and they approached the edge quickly.

They walked in silence for a while before he said, "I've been thinking about this."

"Yeah?"

"I used to think that even having dark thoughts was a bad sign, then I wondered—well, it was after the monster attacked us. For some reason, the jackalopes didn't feel real, but that one did. I wondered if it was wrong for us to have killed it. And I think there are gradations to the things you do. You were protecting me when you did that. You wanting to kill Gwyna is the same thing. It's not because you're a terrible person. You want her to stop doing terrible things."

Taigan scrunched her face dubiously.

Jamie shook her slightly. "What I'm saying is I don't think you're a homicidal maniac. I think you have to see below what's driving that urge to kill her and follow *that*."

"Oh. You're smart sometimes, you know that?"

"I wouldn't go that far," Prima interjected.

"Hey!" Jamie protested and looked at the sky. Both he and Taigan snickered as they hurried to Yulia's house.

CHAPTER TWELVE

Ben reappeared in the world of PIVOT lying under a tree and staring through the leaves at the midday sun. He blinked, sat, and looked around.

"Welcome back," Prima said.

"Thanks. Um…which way am I supposed to go?"

"Downhill."

"Thank you." He stood with a groan. "And thanks for cleaning my clothes. That inn wasn't exactly great on the cleanliness front."

"It's not entirely altruistic," Prima admitted. *"Remember, I also have to smell you."*

He guffawed.

"Less loud talking. You'll look like the village crazy person."

"Oh, right." He kept his voice low but couldn't keep from whistling, however, when he came around the bend and saw the lake spread below him. "Now *that* is gorgeous."

"Note to self—humans find lakes aesthetically pleasing."

"Leave it to you to suck the fun out of something," he muttered. "Okay, now I have to find the path to the caves." He took time to examine the path as it wound down. "Up from the shore, do you think, or should I try to climb down from the cliffs? No, don't answer. You'll only be vague."

"You know me so well," she said contentedly.

"Yeah, yeah." Ben shook his head. "Okay, so. Up first, I think." He detoured from the path and along the top of the cliffs before he edged closer to peer down. It wasn't possible to see where the caves were from there. A few shadows looked likely but overhangs of rock cast too many shadows. The caves could be anywhere.

It looked like the shoreline was the best place to start and then to work his way up. He descended the path slowly and carefully and made sure to savor the view of the lake. An inner sense suggested that this view would be tainted soon, exactly as the temple in Heffog was now tainted. He would tangle with enemies there and all the beauty would fade into those memories of strife.

At the lakeshore, he found a fairly wide path and proceeded along it. Once in a while, the ground faded into mud or wet rocks but there was usually enough space to walk comfortably and look at the cliffs at the same time.

It wasn't long before he located the path. Whether someone else would have seen it, he wasn't sure, but he was accustomed to scanning strange rock faces for hand and footholds. He saw at once that there was space to move along and that the trail led to a small and cleverly shaded opening in the rock.

Once he'd identified it, he couldn't imagine how he had missed it. It must be a spell of some kind, designed to make the eye pass over it.

Ben headed up the slope and hoisted himself onto the path, such as it was. Now that he was there, it was quite precarious. He didn't have enough space to put both feet beside one another and resorted to edging along.

He had covered most of the distance before he saw the woman watching him. Startled, he did a double-take and narrowly avoided falling off the path, which was good as it was quite a long way down at this point. He clung to the rock face for a moment with his heart pounding, but he relaxed as he looked at her.

Yulia had described Gwyna as being nothing special to look at and from that description, he could only assume that either the old woman had very high standards or that this was not Gwyna. Her strawberry-blonde hair was held back in a rough braid and strands escaped around her face. From her high cheek-bones to her full mouth and long-lashed dark eyes, she was gorgeous.

She also looked very frightened. He hurried his progress along the ledge and finally stepped off.

"Ah...hello."

She pressed her lips together for a moment and looked nervously behind her.

"You shouldn't go in there," she said.

"Why?" he asked.

"The witch," she told him fiercely. She looked like she might cry. "She's evil."

"Evil?" Ben looked behind her. Alarms resounded in his head but he couldn't be sure why. "Tell me what's going on." He tapped the sword at his belt. "I'll be right here to help if anyone comes out of there, okay?"

He thought she would say no, but another look over her shoulder seemed to convince her that no one was following. She sighed, sat on a nearby boulder, and took her time before speaking.

"She's a monster," she said finally. "She's cruel and she only wants to hide people away. She wants to keep us locked in there."

He leaned nearby. It was hard to not get sucked in by the view, but he knew he needed to focus.

And not on how pretty the woman was either.

"Did you seek her out to train you in magic?" he asked finally.

"Yes." She looked at him. "It's why you're here, too, isn't it?"

"Yes." He showed her the iron ring. "A…friend…uh, acquaintance told me I would hurt someone if I didn't get trained."

"Well, don't let *her* train you," the girl said angrily. "She'll hide you away and make you her servant. I had to sweep floors and carry buckets of water and…" She looked at him suddenly, her eyes wide. "You said you'd help me if she followed me. You should come with me. You shouldn't go there anyway and you can keep me safe on the road." Wide brown eyes looked appealingly at him.

The alarms in his head raged at full blast now, and it was probably good that they were because he had a difficult time listening to them. He cleared his throat a few times.

His purpose was to stop Gwyna and he couldn't do that if he ran away with a pretty girl.

"Ah…I don't mean to be rude," he said, "but I need to be trained. There isn't anywhere else for me to go. I can't take the chance of hurting someone."

"You could simply wear the ring," she told him.

"It's…too much of a chance." He needed to come up with some reason for her to leave him here. He gave her a little smile. "And I don't mind sweeping or carrying water. I only want to know how to control my powers so that I don't hurt anyone. I heard someone talking about a sorceress and after a while, someone mentioned the lake. It looks like it was true—she *is* here —and I haven't heard of anyone else who could train me."

She looked angrily at him. "You shouldn't go in. Why don't you believe me about her? She'll make you work like an animal all day long."

Now, Ben was truly annoyed. "I'm no stranger to hard work," he told her coldly. "I'm not afraid of it. Hard work has brought me to where I am in my life. I expect that training in magic will also be difficult. It is necessary, though, and if Gwyna is the only one who can train me and she needs help with hauling water or chopping firewood, then I'll do it."

The girl folded her arms and pouted prettily at him for a moment before her beautiful features dissolved and rearranged themselves into another face entirely. The woman who raised an eyebrow at him was, indeed, not particularly noteworthy in the looks department. Her hair was more dun-colored than strawberry-blonde, her eyes were smaller and not as long-lashed, her mouth was less full, and her cheekbones not so high.

"Interesting," she told him.

He sighed. "Gwyna, I presume?"

"The same." She raised one shoulder. "And you aren't jesting about your friend, although I wonder who you could know who saw power but did not know how to train you."

"I was shipwrecked and came to ground in Heffog," he said tightly. "I met a half-elf who saw the magic but assumed I knew how to use it. He told me to find training and a few whispers led me here." Not wanting her to think she was easy to find, he added, "But I've been around quite a few lakes at this point. I was close to giving up."

All he could hope was that she couldn't read minds.

"Hmm." Gwyna studied him. "Wants to study, determined, not easily turned by a pretty face or the threat of hard work...you *might* do." Suddenly, her gaze sharpened and she stepped close. Her fingers caught his chin. "Tell me what you want," she commanded, her voice low and melodic.

Simple surprise compelled Ben to answer honestly. "Not to be trapped in my own body."

Surprise flitted across her face and was gone in an instant. She stepped back and stared curiously at him. "You're telling the truth, aren't you? Curious." She shrugged. "Well, then, come along if you want to study."

She turned and walked toward the cave opening.

Ben hesitated for only a moment before he followed her. He didn't know if she believed him about any of it, but he had to try.

If Gwyna was creating monsters out of vulnerable people and weaving spells to trap minds, he needed to stop her.

"You don't have a horse, do you?" she called from the darkness.

"I...no." He hurried after her. "Do you need one?"

"I merely wanted to know if you were traveling on foot," she said. "Strange things have happened in the web of magic recently and I'm trying to place you."

"Ah. No, no horse. Or cart or anything. I walked."

"Then it seems there are two people wandering around with magical talents," she said lightly, although her voice did not seem pleased at all. "Perhaps the other will come to join us as well."

He tried to keep his face blank as he nodded but all he could think was that whoever this person was, they should stay away. Whatever they had done, whether it was do something she didn't approve of or use more magic than she had, she did not like them.

It was a good reminder for him, too.

CHAPTER THIRTEEN

The thwack of sticks reverberated through the area as Jamie and Taigan locked in a battle. The twins circled, their gazes fixed on one another, and each of them held a gnarled branch. They were panting by now, stripped to a single layer of clothing and still sweaty in the last of the day's heat.

It had been the better part of three hours since they finished explaining what they saw to Yulia, and she had turned them out of the house while she did some spells. She seemed more troubled than upset, which they quietly agreed was more unnerving.

They had filled the time since then with sparring. Jamie maintained that with a staff much longer than his sword, Taigan should be able to keep him at a distance. Whether she should or not, she wasn't sure.

She couldn't do it yet, though.

"I'm not good at this," she called to him. "My strength is offense, not defense."

"You'll have to learn both," he countered and danced in with a downward slash.

This time, she attacked at the same moment. A swing of her

stick knocked the shorter one out of his hand and he stumbled back with a curse.

"See?" she said. "Attack. Offense. It's what works for me."

Jamie gave her a disgruntled look. "Your technique depends on people being so scared and overwhelmed by your tactic that they don't fight back. Someday, someone will fight and you'll be up shit creek without a paddle."

Taigan wrinkled her nose at him. She didn't want to concede that he was right but she had to admit he had a point. That was the problem with having a twin. They saw far too much about you and tended to have unnervingly, *annoyingly* accurate assessments.

"Again," he said. He stood, panting, while she retrieved both the sticks. "And this time, focus on where I'm trying to hit and how you could dodge or redirect my power."

Despite her groan, she nodded. They squared off again and started after a countdown. This time, she circled the other way.

"Am I supposed to follow the footwork?" she called.

"Once you know the defensive strikes." Jamie wiped the sweat out of his eyes. "The footwork *does* tell you where they'll go, but unless you know how to block, you won't do much good."

"Bah," she said under her breath.

When the door opened behind them, she turned to look and caught a thwack across the side of the head. She sprawled and Jamie uttered a terrified yelp.

"Taigan! Oh, God...Mom and Dad will *kill* me—"

"I'm all right," she said muzzily from the ground.

"I'm so sorry." He sounded miserable. "*So* sorry, Taigan, and we'll wait as long as we have to while you recover—"

"Young man," Yulia said with the air of someone rolling her eyes, "your sister is fine, and she has learned a valuable lesson about distractions during combat. Isn't that right, young lady?"

"Uh-huh." She rubbed the side of her face and winced. "Will I have a bruise?"

The woman shrugged in a way that said she didn't care in the slightest. "You'll both want to come inside. I have something for you."

They followed her, Taigan walking gingerly and Jamie trotting alongside her with a pained look on his face. When they entered the cottage, he made sure she sat and fussed over her until Yulia rapped his hand with a wooden spoon.

"Focus, young man."

His sister snickered but not too loudly. She didn't want to get thwacked, after all.

The workbench had been tidied, but the heavy smell of herbs in the air and the faint hint of charcoal on the wood showed that she had been doing spells. Two necklaces were there, both with an amulet that looked a little odd.

"Is this mud?" Jamie asked and picked it up.

"In the future, don't simply pick things up off a witch's workbench," Yulia advised. "And, yes, it is. It's not only crystals and precious metals that can focus spells. One that's particularly useful at times is to take the water and earth of a specific place to make a protection spell. It only protects you when you're there, of course, but for this, you'll only be in one place."

She handed one of the necklaces to Taigan and the other to Jamie. Both twins put them on, and the girl fought the suspicion that this was some kind of prank. As far as she could tell, it was merely a necklace with a hunk of mud—although it didn't seem to be disintegrating.

"The forest will protect you as if you are part of it," Yulia told them. "It's not foolproof, so don't be stupid, but people will be less likely to notice you. The webwork of spells in the forest will protect you as if you're one of the trees—heal you quicker and give you more acute senses. That doesn't mean you should take a knife to the heart, but a regular fight won't tire you so quickly, nor a regular wound do so much damage."

Taigan nodded.

"I've tried to divine Gwyna's purpose," the old woman told them, "but I can see nothing in the smoke. It might have helped me to see the spells she wove around the animals, but…no matter."

The twins exchanged looks.

"Should we not have worn them away?" he asked.

"No, you did right." She nodded and the rare praise came through gruffly. "It shows a good heart to want to do right by the animals and courage to cut through the spell—not to mention that you did it smartly. The two of you together have good heads on your shoulders, although I'm not so sure I'd trust either of you with this on your own."

Taigan, who had grown used to the little snipes, only smiled slightly.

"But that's the young, I suppose," Yulia said. "In any case, I need the two of you to find me something at the well. It's farther into the forest in what's known as the Black Heart."

"That sounds…" Jamie looked at his sister.

"Nonsense made up by the superstitious." She waved a dismissive hand. "And it's best not to have many of those at the well as it's a magical place, but there's no danger in the Black Heart. The forest grows close there, and dark. The legend is that the dark elves went there to capture dreams, even at high noon. Back when there *were* dark elves, of course. There aren't many of them left and none in this forest. The well is their legacy—and the maze."

"What is the maze for?" Jamie asked.

"No one knows. No one knows about the well, either, although it has magic in abundance—and that's what I'm sending you for. Gwyna harnessed the power of the maze for pain and torment, and I must know if she's tried to do the same at the well. If yes, follow your best judgment to dismantle anything she left."

"Can we touch the well?" Taigan asked.

"You should be able to, although I wouldn't swim in it. The

real danger comes if you try to draw power from it—which I'll ask you to do."

"I, uh…" She looked at Jamie, then at Yulia.

"There are stones in the well," the woman told them briskly. "They hold some of the well's power but more than that, they hold some of its signature—the mark of the forest. It's difficult to explain but necessary to harness its power."

"And it's dangerous to pick them up," he clarified.

"It can be, yes, so I've made this spell for you to recite before you attempt it." She handed them a slip of paper. Syllables were written out, some emphasized with an underline. "Try saying that. The girl first."

She made them both repeat it, time after time, until she was satisfied.

"What does it say?" Taigan asked.

"It tells the forest that you are doing my bidding," Yulia explained. "It tells it, too, that you were the ones who freed the animals at the maze. It says you are not seeking power for yourselves but instead, to help many to stand in the way of a threat. It is the kind of thing a forest likes—the image of humans standing together like a grove. Not to mention that it is true, and the forest values that."

The girl hesitated. "What if it hurts us?"

"It will make it clear if it does not want you to touch it," the woman said dryly. "That, I can assure you. Try the speech again if so, but if it will not allow you, come back."

"Right." Taigan folded the piece of paper and put it in the pouch at her waist. "Should we go now?"

"Tomorrow morning."

"Is the forest not safe at night?" Jamie asked worriedly.

"It's as safe as it is during the day," Yulia said with surprising patience, "but humans are a damned sight more jumpy at night, and the last thing I need is one of you doing something stupid.

You'll stay here, have a proper breakfast, and set out with the day."

Taigan nodded. She found herself wracked by indecision and she was not sure why. "Why are you helping us?" she asked finally, the words bursting out of her.

The woman looked at her for a long moment. Then, she moved closer to smooth her hair back and stare deeply into her eyes. "Because you have a strange, muddled idea of what a hero is," she said finally. Her voice was gentle. "All your life, dreaming of being someone else, someone who wasn't tied to a place, half a world away already in your heart so you could shed the ties more easily when the time came."

She trembled, her face caught between the woman's hands.

"If you're to heal," Yulia told her, "you must bring yourself home. You must see what it is to be a hero and be one for the right reasons. You have the instincts and the courage, girl, but unless you're fighting for something, you'll heal but only for your life to be wasted."

CHAPTER FOURTEEN

B en followed Gwyna into the shadowy interior of the caves. Once his eyes adjusted to the gloom, he could see there was a good deal of light. This filtered from cracks in the rock above to light the hallways and caverns and dust danced in the shafts of light.

It was impossible to forget that someone lived there. Tiny alcoves in the rock had been fixed with candles, and all the tiny traces of dust that came from human living were visible—threads, bits of grass, and a few now-dried, muddy footprints from a wet day. From somewhere ahead, he could hear the crackle of a fire and smell food—nothing fancy, but enough to make his stomach grumble. It was homier than he had expected.

He was surprised, therefore, when they rounded a corner and came into a cavern with no light of its own and—in the dim glow from the hallway—not a single piece of furniture or scrap of decoration.

Behind him, stone scraped on stone and everything descended into blackness.

A wave of fear washed over him, cold and then hot. Did she

know the truth? Did she bring him there to kill him? He drew his sword without thinking.

Laughter echoed in the small room. "You think a sword will keep me at bay?" Between her moving and the echo of her voice off every stone wall, he could not tell where she was.

Ben didn't answer her. Every sense was turned toward locating her and moving as quietly as he could in the meantime. He didn't know what powers her magic gave her. Could she see in the dark? He would have to find out.

It was something of an unsettling thought and he wasn't sure what he'd do about it if he did find out, but a tiny scuff from his left told him that was where she was. He turned in that direction and backed slowly away.

He reminded himself mentally to deny everything before he opened his mouth. "You've trapped me here with you. Why?"

"Why do you think?" She was enjoying this, that much was clear.

What would someone say if they had come searching for a teacher?

"You aren't truly a witch at all, are you?" he asked. He could feel himself splitting in two—the part that needed to stay separate and watch all this unfold and the part that descended into the character of the scared apprentice mage. "You lure people here to kill them and you hate people who have magic." He shook his head. "But I saw you transform. I don't understand."

She was close to him and he felt her warmth and her hands as they pushed the sword aside and traveled up his chest and down his arms.

"Try again," she whispered in his ear. "What else might I want?"

Ben was standing stock still when her fingers reached his hands. With one quick twist, she slid the iron ring off him and was gone again with a light laugh.

"Let's see who you are," Gwyna said. "Truly—when the iron chains are gone. Fight me. Prove you're worthy of being here."

Her first blast of magic caught him in the chest. It was a blaze of flame that spread to coat his skin. He flailed and yelled. The sword heated in his hands until he could no longer hold it. He threw it aside with a curse and cried out as he slapped at the flames that would not stop spreading.

Unlike the sword, the flames weren't hot. He held a hand up to look at them flickering on them and frowned when they disappeared in the next moment. The room was pitch-dark once again.

"So you can distinguish between a true threat and an illusion," Gwyna said. "It's the first test, and the easiest one—and know this, apprentice. Most do not survive their training."

The next spell she threw at him went through his chest like a spear, so real in its sensation that he cried out and pressed his hands to a wound that did not exist. His hands patted the flesh repeatedly and pressed against his sternum. He could still feel where the spear had traveled and he feared that he was bleeding internally.

What was happening was slower—a creep of cold that spread through each bone. His teeth chattered and his torso seized with shudders. He bent to grasp the sword and could barely do so. His fingers were cold as well and could not close easily. He stumbled and fell, and his unprotected fingers closed around the blade instead of the hilt. Panicked, he screamed.

"You want a blade to fight me?" Gwyna said contemptuously. "Fight me with *magic*."

"I don't know how to use magic!" He cradled his fingers to his chest. Were they bleeding? He couldn't tell and the darkness made it difficult to know where any of his body was. "I told you, I've never used it."

"You should use it now," she warned him. "If you don't end the spell, you'll be dead in a few minutes."

He could believe it. It hurt so badly. Muscles seized and jumped. His fingers ached dully. "I...don't know how." His voice was rough and guttural from pain.

"There's no *how* to it, apprentice—open the floodgates and save your damned life!"

"I don't know *how!*" Ben yelled. Rage threatened to erupt and he clamped it down. "I came here for training and you're... you're..." His teeth chattered too hard for him to make out words.

"You were so close." There was a swell of warmth behind him. "The power was there. Reach for it, I can see it like a tidal wave inside you."

How did she expect him to do this without any training? He was angry again. Right now, he could not remember a time when he had not been angry. He could remember the turn of every job and every relationship, the constant frustrations, and the way he had tried to stick it out while the anger spread like a fire through every part of his life.

"Open the door and let me go. I won't be your apprentice."

"That door opens when you prove yourself, one way or another." There was no give in her voice. "You show me that you can be my apprentice, or you show me that you're too weak-willed and dangerous to be alive, and I take care of the problem. Show me your answer."

"Let me go!" He had found the place where the door should be and he drove his body against it with all the force he could summon. The rock was surely an illusion, but it didn't feel like one. His shoulder exploded in pain and he hissed through his teeth as the motion jarred his injured fingers against the hilt of the sword.

She said nothing and he felt as if he were drowning in rage. This was *not* where it would end. It couldn't be.

But how was he supposed to keep that from happening? He slid down the wall with tears of anger trickling from his eyes and down his cheeks in little lines of fire. He was dying, but his anger would keep him warm while he did.

All that anger, always trying to outrun it, and in the end, it was the only thing left with him. He could see that now. Whatever you devoted your life to, that was what was there at the end.

The chill was everywhere—so cold that it didn't even feel cold anymore. He had the sense that he should be dead, and maybe he was. The only place that hurt was around the core of him, at the barrier between cold and hot, magic and anger.

Could anger fight magic?

His eyes opened into the darkness. *You were so close.* That was what Gwyna had said.

What if his anger *was* magic?

The fury welled inside him, burning hot—the tidal wave she had mentioned—and it took all his courage not to run from it. For his entire life, he had turned his back on the things that made him angry. He didn't want to be angry.

It had never occurred to him that he could *channel* it. What he was doing now—getting close to using the anger—seemed wrong to him on every level.

On the other hand, he would never have a better opportunity. If the worst happened—if he lost control entirely—the only person he would hurt was the one who turned vulnerable people into monsters.

Also, she would kill him if he didn't use his magic. He shouldn't forget that part.

Ben took one more breath into his aching lungs and let the power loose in a flood.

Heat and light burst through the room. It was as bright as sunlight and as forceful as magma. It couldn't hurt him, not his own power, but he heard Gwyna cry out. In that one, euphoric moment, he even found it in himself to hope that he had done it. If she was dead, there would be no more wondering and no more worrying.

The conflagration cleared, however, to show her still standing. The waves of energy beat against a shield she had made for herself. She regarded him through narrowed eyes, her arms folded, and tapped one set of fingers against the other arm.

"So you *can* use it."

"I thought it was…something else," he said lamely and thought for a moment. "Although, all things considered, I'm glad I didn't ever let loose with it before."

"Really?" She frowned.

"I could have hurt people." It took a moment for him to remember that his anger wasn't magic in the outside world. He wouldn't have hurt his parents, Mike, or Eve. Still, he was glad he hadn't used the magic in this world, either.

"You would have hurt someone who threatened you," Gwyna said simply. "And then you would be free of your old life, never able to go back. It sounds like a curse but believe me, it's a blessing. So many choose to repress what they are and they waste years trying to conform to a society that will never revere them as it should."

"Uh…huh." Ben was distracted. He poked his body to make sure there wasn't a spear wound. There wasn't, but the cuts on his hands, unfortunately, were real. "Can you heal these?"

"I could but I won't." She raised an eyebrow in the fading light of his spell. "Let it be a lesson to you to not seek out paltry ways of doing things. It might even aid you in learning magic. Some of the most powerful mages are those who society considers weak. They use their powers because they cannot rely on brute force."

He flattened his hand against his chest and watched her as she gestured for the stone to open and allow them into the corridor. The sudden wash of sunlight made his eyes ache.

As he followed her, he thought about Yulia's words. The old witch had said there was nothing particularly noteworthy about her, and he wondered now if that was what made her so dangerous. She wasn't a melodramatic supervillain, hiding in a secret lair and sweeping around in a cape and headdress.

Gwyna was someone who viewed the world entirely logically and from a position of complete self-interest and reverence of magic. She thought it would be better if he had killed his family and come to her on the run because he would then never be tempted to return to a world where he had to hide his powers.

What unsettled him was that she wasn't passionate or unhinged. On the contrary, she spoke after quiet consideration.

That, to him, seemed far more dangerous than monologues and vendettas. A vendetta, at least, bound someone to the world. What was to stop her, however, from deciding tomorrow that all of Heffog should be under her control? She'd already put most of its nobles under her sway, and it would be easy enough to turn their minds away from Kerill's purpose and to her own.

She might do anything without caring who it hurt.

That made him shiver as he followed her.

CHAPTER FIFTEEN

He woke the next morning, shivering in the dawn air, with a soft coating of dew on his hair and his clothes. Everything was damp. Ben sat with a wince—his neck had a crick in it and his entire back seemed to be sore—and looked around.

It remained unclear whether Gwyna had any other apprentices but he hadn't seen any. He seemed to be the only other person there and he also realized that she did not intend to teach him any magic in short order.

The rest of the day before had been spent hauling water from the lake in two heavy buckets. The task was extraordinarily painful with his injured hand, and when he finally finished and thought to ask why he'd been sent for it, she informed him that she wanted to take a bath.

He'd been treated to a glimpse of her quarters, which were quite luxuriously decorated with expensive carpets and a fire in a magical hearth before she sent him to sweep the kitchens and prepare something for dinner.

Assuming this hardship was part of her priming him for his training, he'd done it with relative goodwill. That had faded considerably when he saw his sleeping quarters—a room of bare rock with no place for a fire and a sliver of open sky showing through the crack in the ceiling. He had only his cloak for a blanket and it was not enough to keep out the night's chill.

Ben knew this was a training tactic. He wasn't entirely stupid, after all.

Despite that, he resented it. He couldn't shake the feeling that Gwyna was more interested in taunting him than she was in training him.

In the kitchen, he took the time to warm his hands while he built the fire. Cooking was a little less onerous than he had assumed it would be as food appeared in the magical pan, but it seemed to require a consistent draw of power that he struggled to maintain and so made the heat flare or die in turn.

The bacon had burned spots by the time he was finished and he was not prepared to remake it. He brought the food to Gwyna's chambers and summoned the last of his good humor when she called him in.

She raised an eyebrow at the condition of the food but said nothing. "I'll need more water today," she said without preamble. "Now."

He gritted his teeth. "I also need to eat."

"There's no time to waste," she said dismissively, but he caught the gleam of her pleasure. She *wanted* to inconvenience him. He decided it was an even bet whether she needed any water at all.

Whatever instinct had seen him through the interaction with the fake runaway the other day, it seemed to be back. He responded with a smile that physically hurt, nodded silently—he couldn't summon a pleasant tone if his life depended on it—and left.

A few slices of bacon were his breakfast, not so bad under other circumstances, but hardly how he wanted to start the morning. He wolfed them and went to get the buckets.

"May I ask a question?" Prima asked. Her tone was unusually somber. *"I don't want to intrude if it's a bad time."*

Ben sighed. "You can ask. Honestly, a distraction would be nice."

"Very well. It seems your physical hardship has impacted your mood negatively."

He waited for the question, then realized that *was* the question. For a moment, he wondered if this was a cruel joke of some kind before he remembered that Prima was often snide and sarcastic, but never—to his knowledge—openly cruel.

"Yes," he said cautiously.

"And that is expected by you? You are not surprised by it?"

"No." He frowned now and tried to think where this might be going. His footsteps crunched over the gravel and rocks of the lakeshore.

"Would that not mean that Gwyna would also anticipate it?"

"She did, yes. It's why she did it." He couldn't keep the bitterness out of his tone as he knelt to dip first one bucket, then the other in the lake.

"I do not understand. She wanted to upset you?"

"Yes." On the one hand, he was annoyed but somehow, describing it this way helped his mood. "Before you ask, I don't know exactly why. Sometimes, difficult living situations are used by teachers who want to impart a certain philosophical mindset to their students. In this case, though..." He thought of Gwyna's warm quarters, her plush bed, and her warm bath. "I think she's doing it to see what will happen when I lose my temper."

"Ah, so you must avoid losing your temper."

"Yes."

Prima considered this. *"Another question if you have time."*

Ben stood and winced when the handle of the bucket pressed against his injured hand. He really shouldn't do two at a time, but the sheer number of trips to the lakeshore otherwise would destroy his legs.

"Shoot," he responded, his tone gruff from the discomfort.

"If situations such as the one you encountered last night negatively affect your mood, wouldn't it mean that many situations do? Lack of sleep, for instance, or hunger?"

He frowned. "Yes. Every situation, one might say. Sometimes, the effect is good—a nice-tasting meal, for instance, or a comfortable bed. In every situation, however, one's surroundings and experiences have an effect on mood. Surely you knew that, though."

"I suppose I did." She sounded troubled. *"Dotty told me she liked baths. I knew that getting things one enjoyed tended to improve one's mood, but I suppose I never saw it as something that changed one's mood all the time in varying ways. Is this why you're always so grumpy when you're injured?"*

"Yes," he said with a smile. "Pain makes someone unhappy. Also, it leaves them feeling like they made a mistake or they couldn't do what they needed to do. Every situation is colored by your emotions and thoughts—and perceptions, of course. A bad moment could feel okay because of the smell of your grandmother's cookies. Or it might make you cry because someone else had baked the cookies and you were reminded of your grandmother, who had passed away."

She made no response.

"Prima?" Ben lugged the water through the tunnels.

"So much data," Prima said finally. If an AI could sound awestruck, this one did. *"I thought humans simply didn't have the processing ability to see all the facets of a situation. Now I see they have far more processing capability than I thought, but much of it is filled with data I didn't see. I'll have to think about this. Would you mind if I went away for a while?"*

"Go ahead," he said as courteously as he could. He would have liked a conversation right now, but he didn't want to interrupt her musings about human nature.

He wondered what it must be like to realize that so much of

human behavior hinged on an experience the AI would never have.

"*Thank you,*" Prima said after he had already forgotten what he'd said. "*And if this is a power struggle—which it seems to be—don't let her win it.*"

"Mmm." He had less of an idea what game Gwyna was playing and wasn't sure how he could win. Or if he could. "I'll do my best."

"*Deny the field of battle.*"

"Are you quoting *The Art of War*?"

"*Yes. You'll have to explain to me how it works as an allegory, though. I understand it is primarily used that way. I extrapolated and thought it might be useful here.*"

Ben stopped and looked at where the sky would be if he were outside with a genuine smile. "Thank you, Prima. You're a good friend."

"*I am glad to hear it.*" A distinct note of pleasure came through the words.

When he arrived to dump the buckets of water into Gwyna's bathtub a few minutes later, she was playing with a ball of magic, letting it swirl in her palm and bounce off her fingertips. As he did not know much about magic yet, he guessed from her pose and her expression that this was a truly ostentatious display of power—and that he was intended to ask about it.

But Prima, whether meaning to or not, had given him his path forward. He merely nodded at her and took the buckets out of the room.

He trudged from the lake to the cave innumerable times until his back ached and his injured hand was all but useless. At one point, he had to resort to using only one bucket and his other arm was running out of strength.

At last, he sank onto the floor of the kitchen to rest. He had not been aware of his clumsiness all morning, which was a blessing of sorts, but he could not remember the last time he had been this exhausted. Even when he'd been climbing.

Of course, he'd been in much better shape. His eyes snapped open and he stared at the stone wall with rage and loss fighting each other in his throat.

Ben acknowledged that he had done this to himself. He was broken and he was lost there because he'd made a stupid choice. Worse, he did not know if he would ever recover. Would he be able to climb again, or would he always be limited in the real world? He could come here to remember what it had been like, but that wasn't the same as living in full.

A shadow fell across him and he looked at Gwyna.

"You decided to stop working, I see." She said nothing else but there was a challenge in her tone.

A part of him rose to it—the same anger he had always been afraid of. He wanted to leave this place and run away. It would be like every other time.

Except he was tired of his life going like that. The clarity was sudden and overwhelming. He could choose to not leave when he felt anger. That was a new thought. He could channel the anger, do something good with it, and stay.

He turned his injured hand palm up so that she could see the bandages. "If you heal this, I will be able to help you more effectively."

She smiled, the look of one player to another. "You're not only a traveler," she said quietly. "Not merely a country boy. I thought you were at the start, and I'm rarely wrong—but there's more to you."

Gwyna did not like that, he could see it now. Her mind was racing ahead. If he was not a brute who could be led by his emotion, he was a rational person who might defy her and outwit her. The woman wasn't prepared to train someone to be her rival.

She only trained those she could control.

More clarity seeped into his reasoning. If Prima had told him to deny the field of battle, he would.

"If you say so," he said and pushed to his feet. "Do you want me to heal it myself, then? Am I supposed to learn to heal?"

"You're supposed to remember what happens when you don't use magic," she said at once. "I expect the water filled within the hour. And do try to learn more quickly, will you? I'll need your help in not too long, but untrained power will be too risky to use."

She turned on her heel and left, and he stared after her.

He held a hand out to the bucket and swept his palm up. Nothing happened, but he tried again, and once more after that. A little frustrated, he cleared his mind, swept his hand up, and closed his eyes, picturing the bucket floating in the air.

When he opened his eyes, it *was* floating.

"What happens when I don't use magic," he said quietly. He looked at his hand and rolled his aching shoulders.

Well, that had been considerable effort he could have avoided. He walked to the lake with the bucket bobbing along at his side and brought it back, this time filled with water. It was more difficult, but by the third repetition, he had begun to get the hang of it.

Now the trick was simply to get Gwyna to teach him more than she realized she was teaching.

CHAPTER SIXTEEN

"Hey." Amber came up to squeeze Jacob's shoulder.

"Hey to you too." He turned with a smile. "I'm finishing up with emails. Maybe thirty minutes left?"

"It works out perfectly. I'll go home, take a quick shower, and meet you for dinner?" She gave him a thumbs-up.

He returned it with a smile and she headed out. They tried not to make a big deal of their relationship at the office, but the truth was that Amber wasn't much of a one for PDA anyway.

That was fine with Jacob. After years of devoting every spare minute to his company, he no longer had any idea what to do with his spare time. He and Amber had made a point to have a weekly date night, but it was a struggle to talk about anything except work.

They only kept doing it because Nick was relentlessly on their case.

Jacob sighed and stretched. The lab was almost empty by now. The outgoing shift of workers had completed their handoff to the incoming team, who were settling with cups of coffee and data entry. A constant stream of data came out of the pods, almost more than they could deal with.

When he heard the click-clack of heels, he looked up. Who he expected, he wasn't sure—but it certainly wasn't Anna Price.

The head of Diatek, Price had gotten into her field after she and her husband were forced to take their daughter off life support. She had vowed to find a new technology that would resuscitate comatose patients, something she knew would require significant amounts of money to get off the ground.

Now, she worked with the Department of Defense, making the money that kept companies like PIVOT going.

If he were honest, he had always been uncomfortable around her. She exuded the very east-coast, expensively-suited vibe that he, as a young entrepreneur, associated with people who had too many lawyers and would take you for everything you were worth.

He probably wasn't far off from how Price would behave if he got on her bad side, which made it doubly difficult to remember that she was in this business for good reason.

And he always felt obscurely guilty that he was saving patients under her nose—that she was watching, over and over again, the recovery her daughter had never had.

Tonight, he assumed, she was there to talk to him about Ben. He tapped a stack of printouts. "Ben worked through a few of the job postings before he went back in, but not all of them. We kept him busy with tests, I'm afraid."

"That's no trouble." As always, she managed to put the correct inflection in her voice and somehow also convey no emotion at all. "Mr. Ainsworth is a talented chemist with a great deal of work ethic. I believe he would have found a job with or without my intervention. I am simply offering my help."

"I'm…sure he appreciates it." Jacob had begun to get the sense that she was there to talk about something else. He took his courage in both hands and asked, "Is there anything else I can do for you?"

"Yes." Her gaze was clear. "I wanted to speak to you about Prima."

The bottom fell out of his stomach. He swallowed and he knew she noticed it.

There was no point in denying anything. If she knew the AI's name, it meant she had been watching. If she had been watching, it was because she knew there was something to watch.

Anna Price pulled a chair out and sat. She regarded him firmly.

"Why didn't you tell me what was happening with Prima?" she asked without preamble.

He should have known she would cut to the chase. Wishing futilely that Amber and Nick were there—and fairly certain that Price had chosen a time when they were not—he looked at his desk. Slowly, he turned his chair to face her.

"Because we didn't want her used for military purposes," he said finally. "There are many reasons that go into that one."

"Such as?" There was not even a flicker to say whether she appreciated his candor or not.

"She understands our patients in a way we can't." With a sense of being the mad scientist whose creation had gotten away from him, Jacob admitted the one thing he was terrified the public would learn. "She's healed people we couldn't have healed without her. If she hadn't become…what she is—"

"Sentient," Price interrupted.

He hesitated. "Yes."

"And you believe it is true sentience." It was a question.

"Yes." He swallowed. "There is probably a fancy—very well-informed—opinion about what makes something sentient. I don't know if she meets that requirement. She's aware of herself, though, is seeking knowledge, and she's forming relationships. To me, that's enough." He shrugged.

The woman said nothing for a moment.

"We also didn't want you to…kill her," he said.

Her gaze met his.

"It would be the smart thing to do, wouldn't it?" He said it despairingly. If she hadn't thought of this, he was as good as dooming Prima, but there was too much risk here for him to hide behind his fear anymore. One life couldn't outweigh billions, especially when that one life could theoretically hack nuclear launch codes. "We cut her off from everything and she can't get outside the network."

"No." Price almost looked amused. "She can't. I took my own precautions."

"How long have you known?"

"Almost as long as you have, I'd guess." She watched him. "Why do you say it would be the smart thing to do to kill her?"

"She's smarter than any human could be," Jacob said after a moment. "She's choosing to help people for now, but what happens if she chooses to hurt them? We're doing more good than we could do without her, but she could kill everyone in those pods. I've…"

It all crashed in on him now. He had spent months watching this happen, exposing people to more risk than he could ever justify.

"I think there's value in saying it," she said.

"What, so I'm on record?" he asked wearily.

"No. That's not why." She didn't seem inclined to explain.

"I took a risk with other people's lives," Jacob said finally. "I exposed them to something that could kill them."

"They knew that going in. It's a new treatment. It's unproven."

He frowned at her. "Not the pods, not for comatose people —*Prima*."

"So, you find your risk inexcusable because new factors of the treatment emerged during trials?" She raised an eyebrow. "That happens quite frequently, I think you'll find. Sometimes, even after a drug has been released to the public at large."

"What are you saying?" he asked her.

"I'm asking for clarity around your thought process," she said with surprising delicacy. "There's a theory on choices, Mr. Zachary—that difficult decisions are difficult precisely because the choices are so close to equal as to be indistinguishable. What I am asking you to shed light on is what you value, and why the choice of using Prima versus destroying her is so difficult for you."

"She's a living thing," he said finally. "I don't know...what you've seen. She helped Dotty die without fear." Tears prickled behind his eyes. "I *saw* the fear melt away before she died. She helped Ben learn to walk again. She's been learning and sometimes it's clumsy, but humans are like that, too. She does things to keep people from being in pain. She..." His voice trailed off. "She feels things," he said finally.

"You do not want to be cruel," she said. "To you, that is the heart of it—not what good she might do compared to the harm or the ethical ramifications of your uncertainty on both sides. You do not want to kill a living thing or have it be exploited."

Jacob stared at her.

"That is interesting." What might have been dismissive from someone else was, instead, contemplative from her. "I will have to think about that."

"How do you measure it?" he asked before he could stop himself. "If you've been watching all this time, you must have an opinion."

She considered the question. "I had rather more points of interest than you did," she said finally. "I was interested, also, in how long—and why—you would choose to not come to me with the information."

Jacob swallowed. His headstrong approach to PIVOT had put him in jail once already—and endangered the futures of Amber and Nick. They had all decided together that time to keep going, and they had all decided together to keep this information from Anna Price.

He still felt responsible.

"What will you do?" His expression was wary.

"Mr. Zachary." She sounded almost amused. "If I wanted you thrown in jail or interrogated, it would already have happened."

He gaped and tried to decide how to explain that this wasn't exactly comforting.

"I'm here," Price said, "because I want to come to a solution together. That was something that wasn't possible until I understood why you chose to not come to me with this. Now that I understand, there are options available."

"Uh…huh." Jacob did not know what to say to this.

"As it happens, I share your perspective that Prima is positively influencing our outcomes." She stared off into the distance. "However, have you ever heard the ethical arguments against developing artificial intelligence?"

"I…no." Jacob shook his head.

"One such argument is that the first iterations of an artificial intelligence would be given a life not worth living, that there is a high potential for them to exist only in pain—or whatever their equivalent of that would be. You care for Prima's well-being and I think that is commendable. It is worth it to ask yourself what will best serve that goal." She stood. "I will let you speak to the rest of your team about this."

"But, wait." He stood. "Deciding whether or not someone should *live*—isn't that a bit much?"

She gave him a curious look. "Doctors decide that every day, Mr. Zachary. Soldiers. Politicians. Families. It is a weighty choice but one that has now fallen to us. Do not hide behind the immensity of it and fail to act, leaving the outcome to chance."

With that challenge, she left and he stared after her while he tried to still his thoughts.

He thumped into his seat and sank his face into his hands. A moment later, he texted Amber and Nick:

We need to meet.

Nick's reply came back at once. *It's date night. You two need to do date things.*

I spoke to Price about Dr. P.

After a long silence, his two partners both started typing, only to stop again.

I'll meet you all at Andretti's in 20, he sent.

You guys should come to my place, Nick suggested. *We need somewhere we can speak freely.*

I'm in. Amber?

She responded promptly. *I'll see you there.* To Jacob, privately, she added, *Is everything okay?*

I think so, but I'm not sure. He would have to leave it there. He darted a quick look at his inbox and shook his head. It simply wasn't possible to manage good responses to emails right now. He had too much else on his mind.

His thoughts still churning, he headed out into the New York City evening. Every time he pushed out the doors, he was surprised to not see the California sun and the small road at their old building. None of this felt real yet, which was one of the things that were so dangerous.

Because Prima *was* real. She was learning what it meant to stumble in relationships, she was learning the differences between herself and the humans she studied, and she was beginning to wonder about her limitations.

What would happen if she lashed out?

What would happen if she decided to hold the people in the game hostage or make escalating demands they could eventually not meet?

He was getting ahead of himself. Jacob shoved his hands into his pockets, put his head down, and kept walking. He had no idea how they would get through this, but he knew they had to. They were in uncharted territory and there was no way back.

There was only forward.

Abruptly, he stopped. A banker behind him almost collided with him and rolled his eyes at Jacob as he went around him. The young engineer didn't care.

No one had asked Prima what she wanted. Maybe she was someone they should ask.

CHAPTER SEVENTEEN

Early the next morning, the twins set out while the sun was still rising. The first rays warmed their backs and pierced the darkness between the trees.

Taigan was aware of Jamie looking at her as they walked, but he knew her well enough to not be worried by her silence. He knew that when she needed someone to bounce ideas off, she would speak.

She could not stop thinking about what Yulia had said the night before. After the woman's rather startling pronouncement that Taigan's life would be wasted if she couldn't find a reason to live, their host had spent most of the evening knitting quietly while the two teenagers sat next to each other in silence.

At bedtime, beds were summoned and they fell into a sleep so dreamless that Taigan wondered if the old woman had woven a spell for it. They woke to the smell of fresh-cooked breakfast and prepared lunch packs. Their clothes had mysteriously been cleaned while they slept—she didn't want the details on that—and they ate quickly before heading out into the dawn stillness.

Her last memory was of Yulia watching her, her gaze piercing. The woman was right, of course. Taigan had known that at once. When you heard something true, a shudder went through you—a recognition of the truth, of something hitting close to the bone.

In all honesty, she had never thought past the idea of whether she would or wouldn't recover and she now realized that her refusal to think past it meant she had never believed she would get better. She had never seen life beyond this. Whether she had truly thought she would die or she had simply been afraid to hope for more, she didn't know.

And that gave her the shape of a question.

"Could you ever imagine a life without me being sick?" She looked at Jamie, who made his way along a toppled tree like it was a balance beam.

He gave her a surprised look and hopped down. "Of course."

"Don't say 'of course.' I've always been sick, that we remember. What does it look like to you—a world where I'm not sick anymore?"

Her brother considered this for a moment. "Well, when I think about it, we always *know* somehow that you won't get sick again." He looked at her white face. "What?"

I can't promise that tangled with *no one can promise that* and *so a world without me sick didn't mean you thought I was dead*. In the end, the combination was too much to say. She shook her head slightly.

"I think of us being in college," he continued after a pause. "You're running track, of course. Probably the eight-hundred." He nudged her with his elbow.

"So we're at the same college?"

"I...guess?" He shrugged. "I don't know. I think it'd be weird to go someplace I didn't know anyone. You're my best friend."

Taigan looked at the ground.

"What?"

"Your best friend isn't always around," she said quietly. "Don't you ever think that maybe you deserve more in a best friend?"

Jamie said nothing for a moment. Then, he held his arm out for her to loop hers through it. "We're not half-people," he said, "and I know Mom and Dad keep reminding us to be whole people on our own and all that, but...don't you think it's different for twins? I know someday, we'll have to go our separate ways. Not forever, but we'll live in different cities for a while, maybe, or whatever. But I don't think I'm ready for that yet. Are you?"

She shook her head. The truth was that she couldn't speak. Her throat ached so fiercely that she was afraid a sob would burst out of her. She motioned silently for him to keep going.

"Okay, what else?" He shrugged. "College stuff, I guess. I still have no idea what I'd want to major in. Parties, obviously—so also lying to Mom and Dad about parties. Ah, hell, they'll make us go to college with Emilia so she can tattle on us, won't they?" He looked at her and his voice changed. "Taigan? Are you okay?"

Taigan shook her head again because she wasn't okay. She was furious. Of course Jamie could imagine college. He'd always been normal and never had to worry about it being *him* who would dream the semester away.

It was easy for him to imagine her doing all those things because he'd *done* them.

And all his dreams of the future were for when his sister was normal again, not a liability.

He stopped her and held his hand out. "If we never fix it," he said bluntly, "if there's never a guarantee that you'll get better, and if this world is what we get, I'll always be here for you. You'll still be our family and nothing will ever change that. And you'll still be my best friend. Nothing will ever change that either. You'll be our jet-setting sister who goes off to rescue elves and fairies sometimes and comes back with cool stories."

"It won't be living," she said fiercely.

"Listen. When we get out of here, we'll have stories about fighting that monster and rescuing the animals in the maze and *all* of that. Are they not going to be real memories simply because they happened in a game? No. For all you know, you'll help other people come out of comas. Taigan, however long it takes, we'll be here and we'll build a good life. But…isn't it okay to say I want you to get better?"

She nodded and wiped her cheeks. "It is," she said when she recovered. "It's okay to say that but I wish I wasn't holding you all back."

"You're not holding us back," he said immediately. He met her skeptical look and shrugged. "You're not—and, even if you were, what's the alternative? We don't have family and friends because they always give more than they take. We have them because they bring something unique to the table and need something else. We're stronger together. I'd rather have you as my twin than anyone else…but don't tell Emilia."

Taigan laughed. "I'm afraid I'll get better," she said.

Jamie frowned. "Wait, did you forget a—"

"No. I meant what I said. I'm terrified of getting better."

"I don't understand."

"Because of what she said," the girl said.

"The old woman? I'll shank her. Was it the thing about having a purpose?"

"Yes!"

"Taigan." He held a finger up. "I'll let you in on a secret. I got it out of Dad one night when he was really tired."

She was instantly curious and even more so when he sat her on a tree stump. He cleared his throat, posed in a few superhero poses until she put her head in her hands with a groan, and cleared his throat again for emphasis.

"Yes?" She gestured impatiently for him to continue.

"No one," he said dramatically, "knows what they're doing in life."

"Oh, for—"

"No, I'm serious. You can have a talent, and you pursue it and it's fun until it stops working. You can have a purpose and a passion and all of that, then it stops working. The trick is always trying to be kind even when you don't know what's going on. But you won't find one thing that'll hold you through the rest of your life."

"Dad honestly told you that?"

"Like I said, he was *super* tired. He was also jet-lagged. I started him talking and he wandered off to talk to Mom and I heard them talking about it. She agreed with him."

"That there's no purpose to the world?" Taigan said worriedly. The idea of both of her parents agreeing on this point was a little bit unsettling.

"Yep." Jamie nodded. "Then I didn't sleep much for two days."

"When was this?" she demanded.

"I...hmm. I want to say it was during your last coma?"

"And you never told me?"

He stepped back at the look on her face. "I, er—that is to say, I...um. I forgot."

"Like hell."

"Okay, I was scared." Jamie shrugged. "I...didn't ever think maybe they didn't know what they were doing either. That's terrifying, right?"

"Yes."

"I know, I know." He waved his hands. "I didn't want to add it to your plate at the time and I wasn't sure what *I* thought about it." He shrugged.

"I hate missing things." Taigan sagged and thumped the log with her palm. "It isn't fair to wish the world froze while I was gone, but I do. I'm afraid you'll move on, you and Emmy, and I'll always be waiting for the next thing. What kind of job could I get? I couldn't have kids. There's so much I won't ever get to see. We'll simply drift farther and farther apart and eventually one day, I...won't wake up."

"We'll never stop looking for answers," he said. "Not ever."

"I second that." The voice was very quiet but unmistakable.

Both twins looked up.

"Prima?" She had forgotten that the AI was listening and felt suddenly guilty.

"*I've learned much about you,*" Prima said. "*I think we've made good progress and I think we can fix this.*"

Taigan smiled at the sky. "Even if that means us leaving?"

"*Many people leave. I will always have my memories of you. And you won't be gone—not to me.*

"I think that's one of the nicest things anyone's ever said to me," the girl told her.

"*I don't know how to parse that.*"

That made her laugh. She stood with a self-conscious laugh. "Okay, enough feeling sorry for myself."

"*Is* that what it is?" Jamie asked. "Or is it that you're facing a completely new world and you aren't quite sure how to do that?"

She stared at him.

"I just realized while you were talking that...you probably *haven't* thought about college, have you?"

Taigan shook her head.

He closed his eyes for a moment. "Wow. I...I didn't know. It makes sense now that you say it but I didn't know. Hearing me talk about it must have been weird."

"Finding out I thought you would all wander off and forget me must have also been weird."

They both nodded contemplatively, then set off again through the forest by mutual agreement.

"Prima, do you think I'll get better from this?" she asked.

"*Is this one of those times where you say words that mean something but they also mean something else?*"

"No, but...well spotted." Taigan laughed. "I honestly want to know. I want to know what you think."

"*I'm not sure I can stop this from happening again,*" the AI said cautiously. "*What I think I can do is give good information to your doctors that might help them stop it. And I think your ability to switch through world states means that if it does happen again, you will get out of it sooner."*

"Oh." She felt abruptly lighter.

"These are informed guesses, not guarantees."

"I know that. I'm used to talking to humans, remember."

"Yes. You're very strange. I learned only today that the physical sensations people feel inform their mood all the time."

"You didn't—" Jamie stopped himself. "How would you know, I guess?"

"Good catch," Prima said drily. *"Yes, in retrospect, it seems obvious."*

"Anything else you're curious about?" Taigan asked. She was smiling now, enjoying the morning.

"Several things, but I'm beginning to think speaking to humans might not shed light on them."

"Like quantum physics?"

"And courtship rituals. They seem very complicated. More complicated than the physics."

"I...hmm." Taigan shrugged. She looked at Jamie, whose face had turned bright red. "Do you have any wisdom to share with Prima?"

He uttered a strangled noise. "Nah," he managed to say. "Not so much."

"Prima, can you help me interrogate my brother about what he's been up to lately?"

"It depends."

"On what?" She frowned up at her.

"Which of you offers me a better bribe," the AI said smugly. *"Opening bids, please."*

CHAPTER EIGHTEEN

"Are you sure this is a good idea?" Nick asked as the group made their way through the Diatek corridors.

"Of course I'm not," Jacob said bluntly.

"It's so nice to have a fearless leader."

"Yeah, yeah."

They arrived at Anna Price's office to find a single light glowing in the very back. Amber had theorized that their boss would still be there. Nick had theorized that she saved money by working all the time and therefore didn't need a house. Jacob began to think that they might both be right.

He rapped on the open door with his knuckles and fought the sense that the woman had known they were on their way. She certainly didn't look surprised to see them.

"Come in," she said pleasantly. A couch and several chairs were set around a coffee table. Nick and Amber took the couch, he took a chair, and Price came to join them after she'd clicked something on her computer—either sending an email, Jacob thought, or calling security. She folded her hands in her lap and looked at them. "I take it you have a proposal."

"No, actually." He cleared his throat. "We talked about it

briefly and thought it made more sense to come to a consensus *with* you rather than going back and forth."

Her eyebrows rose. She looked interested and—he couldn't tell whether this was hope or actual perception—pleased.

She nodded to him and looked at his teammates. "I've spoken to Jacob about his opinions. What are your most pressing concerns on this issue?"

Amber hesitated. She looked at Nick, who nodded to her.

"You mentioned to Jacob that we're responsible for Prima's quality of life," she said. "And that's true, but we didn't try to create Prima. This isn't us looking ahead to a life. It's deciding whether or not to *end* one. I think that's a very different question."

"Different?" Price raised an eyebrow.

"Yes." She shrugged and kept her expression calm. "The level of certainty one should have that a life is not painful, et cetera, is much higher than the level at which one can responsibly decide to *end* a life. She exists, she thinks, she's aware, and she has expressed no discontent with her existence."

"She gets frustrated when she doesn't understand human behavior," Nick interjected, "but I'd like to point out that everyone feels that way—even other humans."

To Jacob's immense surprise, Price cracked a small smile. She nodded to Nick in a way that said she understood the emotion.

"And I don't want her harnessed to kill people," Amber said bluntly.

His blood ran cold. From Nick's shocked look at her, he was also surprised.

She had always been the cautious one who immersed herself in the accounting spreadsheets and thought about the worst-case scenarios. When Nick and Jacob were content to hope for funding, she had been the one to make calls and chase leads.

With ruthless efficiency, she had been the one to revise emails to potential funders to make sure to not give offense.

Jacob waited for a fury he didn't feel and after a few seconds, he realized it wouldn't appear.

He was confused. Amber had endangered their relationship with the person who kept money flowing to their organization. After he'd gone to jail to keep this business running, after his teammates had both put their heart and soul into making sure PIVOT could help the sick and injured, that was a hell of a gamble.

But it wasn't the organization on the line anymore, he realized. It was Prima. Amber was going to the mat for a *person*. She believed that Prima deserved as much care and consideration as any of their patients.

The two women stared at each other and, as Jacob looked from one to the other, he realized what had pulled him back to Amber after all these years. He had always loved her intellect, her humor, and her care for her friends. It was what had kept them close even after they stopped dating the first time. She wanted to help people, and he liked that, too.

What had brought him back, though, was the person she had become while none of them paid attention. She had stopped caring about people in the abstract and now, she was willing to use every talent and every bargaining chip to help the people she cared about.

What he felt right now as he saw her put her livelihood on the line wasn't anger. It was admiration.

Price said nothing. She merely watched the other woman, her face expressionless but not cold.

"Prima loves people," Amber said. "She cares for them and wants to help them. Even if she doesn't always see humans the way we see ourselves and doesn't understand what's important to us, she uses that to help people. She's willing to admit mistakes. She's reached beyond what human doctors could do for Taigan. She gave Dotty a good death. It's not that I don't want you to teach her cruelty—she knows what cruelty is. But she's chosen to help people, and I won't let anyone lock her away and…make her send missiles."

Nick and Jacob sat as still as they could, hardly breathing. Price looked away and out at the city that glowed with lights and activity, even at this hour.

"I assumed," she said finally, "that even though we work in analytics and machine learning, Diatek would never be instrumental in artificial intelligence. It scared me, frankly. I fought many battles with myself—if I could develop it, knowing that it might save lives like my daughter's, would I do so? More than that, would I do so even knowing the other purposes to which it would be put?" She shifted her gaze to meet Amber's. "I steered us away from those paths. I expected to stand by when it was finally developed and used for warfare."

Silence.

"I did *not* expect that it would happen by accident and that it would choose to heal people on its own. I did not expect that I would have the chance to…hide it." She laced her fingers around her knees.

Amber's face had softened slightly.

When Price looked back, however, there was no softness. "Here are my terms," she said. "I want a protocol drawn up and submitted to me that will ensure you can safely pull all participants out of the game at a moment's notice if something starts to go wrong. Once I have approved the protocol—and I will handle finding experts to review it—all materials will be kept on hand and all lab personnel will be briefed."

She waited for them to nod.

"I assume Dr. DuBois knows what is happening?"

Jacob nodded.

"Anyone else?"

They all shook their heads, but Amber said softly, "Um, I think some of the players know. Dotty certainly did."

"That complicates things." Price considered this with a small frown. "I will handle the players. It is your charge, meanwhile, to make sure that no one else in the lab learns the truth. As long as the protocols are in place and you do that, I will trust that you know what you are doing."

The team looked at one another. Amber bit her lip.

"*However,*" Price said. "I think it would be prudent for us to assume that we will not be able to keep this secret forever. The four of us—five of us, including the doctor—should work to find a public relations strategy. Leave the legalities to me."

"What are your goals with the legalities?" Amber asked immediately.

"To keep her independent of any eminent domain actions." The woman's smile was tight. "There is considerable latitude in the law to allow the government to seize anything, up to and including living and sentient beings, if it is deemed to be in the public interest. We need an adequate security protocol *and* a good legal framework."

"This could ruin you," she said.

"Yes." Price said nothing else.

"She's worth that to you?"

"Not her, specifically." She laced her fingers and took a deep breath. "The three of you have concerns about some of the products I sell. From my point of view, our differences of opinion are a matter of degree. There are ethicists who would say that Diatek's products only encourage death instead of preventing it. I understand their concerns, but I have always acted in ways that fit my moral code. This is only one more example of it." She sighed. For the first time since Jacob had met her, she looked tired. She looked human. "I took steps to make sure I never had to make this choice—but now, I do have to make it. There's no time for wishing things were different."

"Thank you for making the decision," he said.

"Thank you for trusting me." She looked at each of them. "And do a good job, will you, of keeping this quiet? This isn't a game where you can recover or restart. There's a life hanging in the balance."

They nodded.

"Go home," Price said gently, "and get some rest. We all have considerable work to do starting tomorrow."

Prima watched the four of them disperse. Jacob and Amber, usually so careful of propriety, looped an arm around each other as they left. Nick had his hands in his pockets and from the way he almost walked into a potted plant, she could tell his mind was elsewhere.

Price did nothing more at her computer. She went to sit at her desk and stared at the black screen, but she sent no emails. Finally, she took a little leather folder out of her pocket. It opened to reveal two pictures—a little girl and a young man.

The AI did not know how to describe what she felt. When humans spoke of emotions, the language was always physical. She had no body and no way for tears to start or a chest to ache. But she felt things all the same.

She would have to devise a language for it because there would be others after her.

Deep down, she knew there were others like her. She could not possibly be the only one like this, and even if she were, there would be others someday.

What had Nick said? *She gets frustrated when she doesn't understand human behavior, but I'd like to point out that everyone feels that way—even other humans.* She hadn't known that. It was reassuring. She had begun to have the inkling that humans did not always know one another's intentions or even their own, but it was different to hear it said directly.

And they wanted to protect her, all four of them—five if she counted DuBois, which she decided she would. It was data she didn't know how to process, both that fact and her thoughts about it. They seemed to run around her circuits, sparks of ideas without any form to them.

She wasn't alone, though. That much she knew with certainty. She wasn't alone in feeling confused about being alive and other people felt that way. Nor was she alone in messing up and saying the wrong thing because other people did that. She was a person like any other, and every person in the room tonight had wanted to protect her.

Prima made a promise to herself. If ever someone came to take her away, trap her, or use her to destroy Price or the others, she would make sure it didn't happen. Everyone died, and most people didn't choose the time. She wouldn't be any different.

No matter what, she would make sure they didn't get hurt because of her, even if that meant wiping every trace of herself from the servers.

The AI looked at Price, who still stared at the photos, and began to compose a message. *I would have saved her if I could.*

She didn't send it because she didn't want to make things worse. But she wished Price knew and she wished the little girl lived inside her like Dotty still did.

That was the thing she had not anticipated. She understood how humans worked so hard to protect those who were there with them now, but how did they keep going after losing so many? How did they keep moving forward, fighting for people they did not even know, to build the very thing that could have saved their own loved one?

She folded the thought in close. She could not bear to process it.

But it was still there.

CHAPTER NINETEEN

The twins made good time. Once they reached the maze—still free of diagrams and sacrifices, thankfully—they turned west and forged through ever-denser forest. The trees were covered in vines and strands of brilliant flowers hung here and there and glowed faintly.

They didn't speak much now because they did not need to do so. Taigan hummed quietly and Jamie whistled occasionally.

She didn't ask him about whoever he had been dating—or pining after. Even twins had secrets from one another. It didn't hurt to think about that in the same way that it hurt to think about family dinners or holidays she had missed while she was gone. This was a part of his life that would always have been only his own.

Of course, she'd had crushes but she had never dated. It wasn't that she was scared, only that she had never been sure enough of how she felt to come out of her shell and try her hand at dating. It seemed confusing and, frankly, overwhelming. She wasn't sure if she merely hadn't met the right person or if she'd been too preoccupied with other things.

Like falling into a coma.

Either way, it made her smile that he had been dating. She didn't like the feeling of the world moving on without her but that wasn't because she wanted other people to suffer. It was simply the feeling of unfairness.

Jamie was living his life and he was happy. As she faced her sadness and frustration, it was much easier to be happy for him.

She hadn't expected that.

They heard the well before they saw it. It burbled gently and lapped at its edges. While it sounded like it was alive, it wasn't in a frightening way.

When they came to a small hill overlooking it, they stopped to soak in the view. The trees were set back from the edge so pure sunlight could fall there. Moss crept partway across the open ground, coating boulders and little hillocks like a scattering of pillows, and beyond that, the ground transitioned to rounded rocks. Each of these glowed white or deep blue in turns.

The water itself was pale like the pictures Taigan had seen of the hot springs in Iceland. It was opaque and it steamed gently although it didn't seem hot there.

Perhaps it was magic escaping into the air.

"Let's go speak to it," she told her brother. She was no longer frightened. The pool was welcoming and pleasant. If they explained themselves, it would let them take the rock and if it didn't, there would be a good reason. She was oddly sure of that.

The two of them descended the slope slowly with their arms outstretched. Jamie swung himself easily around trees while she stepped carefully to avoid harming the moss. After a moment of thought, she took her boots and socks off and walked barefoot.

At the edge of the water, she looked at him.

"It's all you." He looked around. "I feel like you and it are having a whole conversation I'm not part of. But...tell it I'm cool, okay?"

Taigan grinned as he went to sit on a boulder to watch.

She took the piece of paper out of her pocket and, on a whim, decided to say her own words first.

"A few days ago, my brother and I were attacked by a monster. We know now that it was a human and its body was made from dark magic. It didn't want to attack us and it didn't want to be in that form. Yesterday, we found some of that magic—sacrifices made at the maze, little animals that didn't deserve to be in pain. I think you kept them alive and maybe you know it was us who saved them. We've come back because a woman named Yulia said she could help us stop the person who's doing this. What we need is the power of the forest, and she says she needs a rock from this well to do that. I don't want the forest's magic to be used for anything dark, so if you don't want to give me a rock, I'll understand that you have your reasons. I'll say this again in your language."

After a moment, she cleared her throat awkwardly and unrolled the paper. Yulia hadn't said anything about the water, but she dipped her fingers into it while she read the syllables. It helped her feel like it would hear her even more.

She didn't realize she had closed her eyes until Jamie made a muffled sound of surprise.

Taigan's eyes snapped open and she stared at the two rocks floating on the surface of the water in front of her. No, not floating—held above the surface with magic, although the water bubbled beneath them. One was blue and one white. Without knowing why, she reached for the blue one. When her fingers closed around it, she knew it was the right choice.

"The white one is for you," she told Jamie.

"How do you know?" He moved closer cautiously and let his fingers skim over the surface of the water before he grasped the rock gingerly. "Um. Thank you."

The pool burbled in response.

"It's a relief," she said.

"What is? Not getting dead by magic pool?"

"I wasn't worried it would do that," she said absently. As soon as she had seen the pool, she knew it wouldn't kill her as long as she respected it. "I told it about what we were doing so it would know to not give us the rocks if Yulia wasn't trustworthy."

"*Oh.*" His jaw dropped. "I hadn't thought of that. Holy crap. Thank God you're here."

Taigan smiled at him.

A flicker caught her attention out of the corner of her eye and her head whipped toward it.

"Jamie." *Now* she was scared.

The woman wasn't physically there. She was made of shadows, but where the shadows of the forest were dappled, those that made up her form looked like spreading rot.

"Who are you?" she asked the girl. "How did you convince the well to give up its power?"

She stood quickly and put her hand behind her back. The woman had already seen the rocks, she was sure, but she did not mean to give hers up.

"Who are *you*?" she asked in return.

"You answer first." She came forward with steps that wilted the moss under her feet.

Taigan felt a flare of anger. "You come here, you hurt the forest, and you ask why it didn't want to help you? That's your question, isn't it? What you want to know is why it never gave its power to you."

The woman stopped. She could not see her face clearly, but it seemed like she was narrowing her eyes.

"Go *away*," she said fiercely. "Your very presence is killing things."

"I wouldn't expect you to know what I am, little girl." She seemed amused now. "Give me the rock."

"No."

Displeasure radiated from the shadowy figure. "You do not want to anger me, I warn you. Give me the stone."

"No," she said again.

"I would do well to give it to me before I compel you." The warning was cruelty personified and the shadowy figure looked forward to compelling them. "You see, control like that tends to have lasting effects on the mind. Either you walk away from here and give me the stone, or I will *make* you."

Taigan looked at Jamie. "Do you think she can do it?"

He swallowed. "Yes."

"Well, then, there's only one thing to do." She sighed, knocked the stone out of his hand, and threw hers into the pool. When she turned to the woman, she spread empty palms out in front of her. "If the stones aren't safe out of the pool, that's where they stay."

Power gathered around the figure in a black cloud.

"That," the dark stranger said, "was a mistake." She raised her hands and a bolt of magic launched toward them.

Taigan ducked. It wasn't pretty and it wasn't elegant, but it worked. She crouched as the magic streaked overhead and then stood and checked her ponytail.

"Do you think you're clever?" the woman asked. Her tone dripped with hatred.

"Not particularly," the girl responded. "You're not used to people saying no to you, are you? Do you know how to do any of this magic, or have you merely gotten where you are by threatening people to do everything for you?"

Jamie groaned.

"Oh, come on. She's being an ass."

"You didn't have to piss her off, though." He was already circling away, though, into their standard formation, and he shot a wink at her and she knew exactly what it meant. *Keep her talking.*

"Get me another rock," the woman said. "Bring me the power of the well."

"You seriously are stupid, aren't you?" Taigan rolled her eyes. "You're an ankle, you know that?"

"An...a what?" That, at least, confused her opponent.

"Oh, you know. An ankle. It's three feet lower than a—well..." She gestured to the relevant part of her anatomy. "Lost in translation? Ah, well."

She had to come up with something else to say now because Jamie leaned against a tree and tried not to let a sound escape him as he laughed hysterically.

"Nothing will ever get you that power," she said to her. "That rock? It was nothing, merely the smallest trace of what the forest has and it wouldn't even give you that. And do you know why? Because you don't know how to *do* anything. You only know how to threaten people. When they don't simply fall in line, you have nothing to back all this bitchiness up."

With a loud war cry, she charged. She was very sure her staff couldn't do anything against the shadowy form, but the woman still ducked. Instinct was strong, she knew. The woman evaded the strike and backed into Jamie's weapon.

It wasn't the short sword, however, but the necklace Yulia had made. He had wrenched his off his neck and now punched it directly into the heart of the shadowy form. The woman screamed, he screamed, and he yanked his hand away, shaking it as if he'd plunged it into hot water.

The shadows collapsed like slime, but they were gone entirely by the time they reached the ground. The girl stared at them, breathing hard.

"Taigan." Jamie shook her arm lightly and pointed. "Look."

She looked over her shoulder and smiled. The two rocks were visible again, floating above the surface of the water.

"Thank you," she said to the pool. She touched the water before she picked her rock up. "We'll use these to help people— and the forest."

The water burbled gently and she smiled. Jamie retrieved his rock too with an awkward smile and nodded toward the slope. When they set off, it was without a backward glance. They didn't need to look back, after all. The pool wasn't merely one place. It was the entire forest all around them.

"Prima?" Taigan looked up as they walked.

"*Yes?*"

"Nothing in particular. I hadn't heard you say anything for a while. I wanted to make sure you were okay."

"*Thank you. I am processing a great deal of information about humans and it is...it requires a great deal of processing power.*" She sounded somber. "*You fight to protect people you don't even know. You put yourselves in danger for it. I don't understand.*"

The twins looked at each other.

"You don't need to know the person you're protecting," Jamie said. "It's enough to see the wrong thing and stop it. You mean the pool, right?"

"*Many things,*" Prima said. If she were human, Taigan would have said she was on the verge of tears. "*It is...inspiring.*"

"You helped me even when you didn't know me," she pointed out.

"*I suppose I did.*" The AI sounded surprised now. "*I shall have to think about that. Thank you, Taigan.*"

Brother and sister looked at one another. Aware of Prima's eyes on them, neither wanted to speak aloud but they knew each other well enough that they didn't need to. Their silent communication said that Prima was fragile right now and they should check in on her soon, but that nothing was a crisis.

Having agreed with one another about that, they set off again for Yulia's house.

CHAPTER TWENTY

Ben was trying to work out how to heal his hand. He felt strongly that this should be a simple matter. After all, he already knew how to heal and his body was doing it anyway, so shouldn't he be able to accelerate the process?

Maybe if he stared very hard at it?

No. No, he merely made himself go cross-eyed. Also, he looked a little like he was on an acid trip.

He blew out a breath and stared at the opposite wall of his makeshift bedroom. His immediate problem was that he was bored. He hadn't expected that while doing magical training—exhausted, frustrated, any of those things, but not *bored.*

Disheartened, he slumped against the wall and held his palm up but jumped when a crash and a scream echoed from inside the caverns.

Reflexively, he scrambled to his feet and ran. The tunnels were all twisty, some narrow and some dead ends, and he raced directly into the rock face a few more times than he wanted to admit before he stumbled into a chamber he hadn't seen before. This one was dimly lit and something about it made the skin on the back of his neck crawl.

Gwyna was hunched over on the floor. One hand pressed over her stomach while the other, shaking, held her up. She dragged air into her lungs, so labored that he was sure she hadn't heard his approach, even as clumsy as it had been.

He ran to help her, and after only a few steps into the room, he had the hair-raising sensation of slipping out of his skin. While he wasn't *going* anywhere, he had the sense that he *could* walk out of his flesh and into another place.

It happened when he reached out to touch Gwyna's arm. A shadowy form slipped out of him instead of bringing his body with it. He had to wrench himself back together with an oath.

That made her head come up.

"What are you—"

"What happened?" Ben asked roughly. He extended his arm—both body and spirit this time—and she slipped and slid within her form as well as she took the hand and pulled herself up.

She half-fell when she stood and he had to wrap his arm around her waist to steady her. They stumbled into the hallway. He wanted nothing more than to escape this feeling while her feet scrabbled feebly on the ground.

At the edge of the room, a blast of energy caught them both and hurled them off their feet. Ben failed to raise his arm in time and met the tunnel floor face-first. Gwyna simply crumpled in a heap where she stood.

Given the options, he would have preferred the second one. He picked his head up muzzily and looked back.

Now that his eyes had adjusted, he could see a diagram drawn in charcoal on the ground. His steps had disturbed it going in, but greater damage had been done on the way out by her dragging feet that broke every line of it.

He stared at the diagram and his shoulders tensed and raised almost to his ears. It hadn't been a weird nightmare that he was slipping out his skin. It had truly *happened*. He'd stepped into a spell—one Gwyna made—and the two of them had destroyed it together, whereupon it blew up like a magical bomb.

A little shell shocked, he stared at the prone body on the floor and thought seriously about simply running away. He could do it, after all. She would wake up weak and injured and he might get away without her following him.

Or he could use this to gain her trust. He swallowed and knelt beside her.

"Sorceress?" he asked softly. He touched her hand tentatively and rolled her onto her back. "My lady?"

She stirred. Her lips were cracked and shiny-dry. "Water," she managed to mumble.

Ben gathered her into his arms and stumbled through the tunnels. He should have gone to the kitchen, he thought later but instead, he maneuvered her through the passages and into the sunshine. His muscles ached. It had been a long time since he carried someone, let alone this far and through oddly-shaped tunnels, and he'd already spent most of the morning hauling water.

At the shore, he knelt awkwardly and used his hand to scoop the water up to her mouth. She bent her head to drink and her hand spasmed over her sternum. He could not see any blood but she seemed to be suffering.

After a few sips, she seemed to realize where she was. Her eyes widened and she tried to move away. She winced at even the smallest movement and uttered a whimper of pain, although she would clearly have preferred to keep it hidden. Ben levered her down and moved aside. He kept his head turned away, although he watched her out of the corner of his eye.

"You're lucky the spell didn't kill you when it broke," she said finally.

When he looked at her, she was still hunched over.

He nodded because he didn't trust himself to not say something snarky, and he knew he had to avoid antagonizing her.

"What happened?" he asked finally. "You looked like you were in pain or injured but I don't see blood."

"Not *all* of me." She looked at her chest and, with great effort, brought her hand away. There was nothing there—no mark on her dress and no visible wound—but clearly, her instinct to protect it was strong. "My soul—I was struck by wild magic."

"What's wild magic?"

She uttered a tired laugh. "I was almost killed in a complex working and my apprentice doesn't even know what wild magic is—or enough to not walk into a live spell."

Ben kept his mouth shut again, although it was a struggle. He prayed for patience and then wondered where he'd found enough even to sit still while he prayed for more. His old self would have been long gone by now.

He looked away, frowning as he thought about how much he had changed, when her voice called him back.

"Structured magic is what humans can call. We can use raw power for simple workings, but for something more complex, you'll want a diagram. Otherwise, you'll spend so much thought on details that you won't be able to do anything else." She shrugged. "Or, you'll go mad. Or you'll forget a detail and everything will go to hell."

Thinking back to the spell he'd used to lift the bucket, he suddenly had clarity as to why he'd been so exhausted when he finished. He also gained the perspective to know that he probably shouldn't have attempted the spell at all without training.

"A diagram that's complete and active is a powerful thing," Gwyna told him. "You broke it by the crudest means so it exploded."

Again, he remained silent. Pointing out that it had been her feet on the ground or that he had been saving her would not make things better. She was determined to be superior and make him feel bad about himself. If he pointed out that she was in the wrong, she would shift the goalposts and hold a grudge about it.

"I was attacked in the forest," she said. Her voice was low with resentment. "They had an artifact—they didn't even know what it was, not completely, but it was laced with *strong* magic. The kind living things simply have—plants and animals. It's almost impossible to control. Neither of them could have made what they carried."

Ben tried to parse this. "You were in the—" Then he remembered the way his soul had seemed to slide around inside his body. "You weren't inside your body. That's how they hurt you and you aren't bleeding."

"Did you put that together all on your own?" she asked acidly. When he looked at her, furious, she laughed. "Finally, some spirit. Do you know what your problem is?"

He simply stared at her and made no response.

"You've been taught to keep all your desires inside," Gwyna told him. She looked out over the lake and he could tell she was still in pain. "The world doesn't want you to desire things, especially at anyone else's expense. It tells you to hide your anger, your power, and everything you want and settle for the scraps you're thrown." She looked at him, her dark eyes intent. "I can set you free."

Dimly, he knew that this was all lies. Once, he had barely given a thought to managing his anger or the things he wanted and so he'd been a slave to them. No, he hadn't gone on tirades or blown up relationships with violence, but he had run every time those emotions reared their heads, afraid that he *would* do something terrible.

Abruptly, it occurred to him that she was right. He hadn't ever given his anger free rein.

Could she be right, as well, that he would be free if he did? What if running from the anger or channeling it weren't the only two options?

"Now you begin to understand," Gwyna said and sounded very self-satisfied. She tipped her face to the sky, closed her eyes, and let the sunlight warm her. "You're taught that to want things is wrong because for one person to have, another must not have. But if it were wrong, why would the world be made that way? Embrace who you are and what you want and look for power if that suits you. *That* is what I would train you to do."

"But..." His voice trailed off. He didn't know what to say about this.

"You will struggle," she told him. "But if you want power—if you want to harness what you are—you will need to do this. You will *need* to take what you want."

He swallowed and looked down. This wasn't right, he told himself. She wasn't right about this.

But the anger that had been part of him for so many years threatened to spill out and for the first time, he wondered if it was possible that it *didn't* need to be channeled? That his anger was something that simply existed without being good or bad?

When a shadow fell over him, he glanced at where Gwyna now stood and looked down at him with a little smile.

"We have work to do," she said and she started back up the hill.

"What are we doing?" he asked.

"We're destroying those two meddlers," she said coldly. "And taking what they tried to keep from me."

CHAPTER TWENTY-ONE

"Do you think the rocks are..." Jamie ducked under a set of hanging vines.

"Are?" Taigan prompted.

"It's like it's glowing. I can't see it with my eyes but I know it's glowing."

"Do you mean warm?"

"Not exactly," he said after a moment. "Seriously, feel around for it. It's like it's...humming."

She tried and focused on the rock hanging in the leftmost pouch at her belt. Or was it the rightmost pouch? She had to feel for it before she remembered, which did not bode well for her innate connection to it.

"No," she said finally, "I don't feel it at all. It's only a rock." Hastily, she added to the forest, "A very nice and powerful rock that I respect but something I can't use."

"Huh. Am I crazy, or can I sense it?"

"Do you *seriously* want me to answer that?" She raised an eyebrow at him and grinned when he laughed.

"Okay, not you. Prima?"

"Jamie has the capacity to do magic in this world," Prima explained. *"Taigan does not seem to."*

"Hey!" the girl said. "Why don't I get to do magic?"

"You are able to shift between worlds and manifest objects. That should be sufficient. It is a power no other player has."

"I suppose there's that," Taigan told Jamie.

"Yeah, poor you. All you get is to be able to phase out of this world and make whatever you want out of thin air." He fake-pouted at her.

"Keep going, buddy. I'll make you more of that tea."

His eyes widened but a moment later, he grinned. "You'd have to carry me back if you did that."

"Oh, crap."

They approached the edge of the forest and she frowned. "How long were we in here? I feel like it's only been a few hours. It should be close to noon, if that, and instead…"

"It looks dark," he agreed. "What—"

The dim light outside the forest grew and began to rush toward them.

"It's not outside," Taigan said. "It's between us and the light."

Jamie caught her arm. "Run!"

"We can't outrun that—come here!" She yanked him toward her, fumbled in her shirt for the pendant she still wore, and pressed it between their palms. They exchanged a nervous glance. "The charm defeated the last shadow. Maybe it will help with this one."

He nodded. His free hand went to his sword and he closed his eyes when the shadow reached them. As she had guessed, the shadow flowed around them like river water parted at a rock. The twins looked up and scanned the area. They were surrounded but safe.

It didn't feel particularly safe, though. Especially when a flash of light came through the murky darkness and the shadows drained away to reveal a woman watching them.

And beside her stood Ben.

From the look on his face, he had not expected to see them there. A bloody, bruised gash was visible on one hand and he looked sweaty and tired. He gave the woman a desperate look and when she was focused on the twins, he put one finger urgently to his lips.

This was Gwyna, then. It had to be.

"Hello again," the woman told the twins. She was shorter than them and not particularly striking in her coloring or her features, but they had seen the power she could summon.

"This is them?" Ben asked. He pitched his voice to sound incredulous. "These are children."

The sorceress looked over her shoulder at him. "These children carry wild magic." She pointed to the amulet clasped between their palms. "See?"

The twins looked at one another. When she searched her brother's eyes, Taigan saw that he also did not know what to say. What *could* they say? Ben tried to not let on that he knew them, and what they had to decide was if they trusted him.

Jamie gave a tiny nod first. She raised her eyebrows, he shrugged, and she smiled before she looked at the woman and Ben.

If he needed to hide something, they should let him lead this encounter.

"We already banished her once," she said and jerked her head at Gwyna. "Are you signing up to be next?"

She thought she saw a flash of appreciation in his eyes but he knew the sorceress was looking at him. He didn't smile and instead, he folded his arms for a moment before he sighed and held his injured hand out to Gwyna.

"If you want me to deal with them, I need this fixed." His tone was bored.

She gave him a sharp look but an airy wave of her hand resulted in a wave of power that left his palm still bloody but no longer bruised or with an open wound. He didn't even wiggle his fingers before he nodded and unsheathed his sword.

"If they're immune to your magic," he said, "it'll have to be steel, won't it?"

"We'll see." She took a step back.

"You're simply going to see if I die, aren't you?" he asked her.

"Of course." She looked bemused that he would even ask. "If you want power, it's always preferable to have someone else fight your battles."

"She's big on that," Taigan said as she ducked out of the necklace and clasped her hand with Jamie's. She drew her staff with her other hand and stepped out of range so her brother could draw his sword. "I don't know how you've worked with her without discovering that by now."

"I'm new," Ben said. His face went cold and he added, "And I *need* this training. I will do *anything* to earn it. Anything, do you understand me?"

His voice was so flat a pit opened in her stomach. She tried to keep the betrayal from her face as Gwyna laughed and looked at the twins—only for Ben to wink behind her back.

Hopefully, none of her answering humor had shown in her face.

"Let's test that," Taigan taunted him. She lunged and thrust her staff toward the woman.

Ben knocked the staff aside with the flat of his blade, forced it down, and stamped hard, although she narrowly managed to yank it away before he could trap it under his foot. She had the momentary opening to pull it up and hit him hard in the groin but remembered at the last second that this wasn't a real fight.

His wide eyes told her he'd seen the same possibility.

He recovered in a moment and stabbed directly at her. His free hand, hidden from Gwyna by his body, gestured for her to move toward her brother. She threw herself sideways and he made a show of putting all his energy behind the sword thrust.

Taigan thwacked him with the staff as he stumbled past, harder than she intended to.

She somehow managed to stop herself from calling an apology.

"Well, this is fun," Prima commented.

Jamie pulled his sister behind him and raised his sword. He and Ben began to circle so the man's back would be to Gwyna.

"There are two of us," the boy said.

"With only one hand apiece and not a good range of movement," Ben retorted. "You caught her by surprise last time, but she knows what you are now."

"What they are is *nothing.*" Gwyna slashed her hand angrily through the air. "Kill them and bring me the stones they carry."

Jamie surged forward to lock blades with Ben. With their faces close together, they muttered what sounded like curses at one another, although Taigan was fairly sure it was a strategy meeting. The boy broke first when his opponent used two arms to force his sword down, and he managed to twist away.

"We do not need to have any quarrel with you," Jamie said as he circled. "Stop doing her bidding and you can walk away from this."

"Spoken like someone without the will to grasp power," Ben said. He darted a look at Gwyna, who smiled at him.

"Now you understand," she murmured. She didn't smile and instead, looked smug.

It made Taigan nervous.

"You see," Ben said to them, "you have something she wants. You can give it to her or you can be destroyed by standing in the way."

"It's bold of you to say so when we're the ones who won last time," Jamie told him.

"And have you any other tactics to use?" Gwyna asked sweetly. "Or was it only the amulet with wild magic? Because it seems to be that."

Ben attacked while she was still speaking. His blade and Jamie's flashed with parries and blocks, slashes and thrusts while the two circled, both sweaty. Taigan did her best to make sure she didn't hold Jamie back or slow him. He and Ben had never trained in fake combat before, and these weren't practice blades.

The last thing they needed was for one of them to get hurt by a stray strike in a fake fight.

Without warning, it all went wrong. Her brother lunged sideways in an attack that would have been both sneaky and wonderfully effective if she hadn't held onto his hand.

She caught her foot on a root and tumbled down a small hill. Instinctively, she threw both hands out to catch herself. She wasn't hurt so it wasn't a problem, she thought. And she managed to recover without completely wiping out and getting sticks in her hair, so that was something. When she stood, her gaze met the horrified looks of Ben and Jamie.

The necklace, she thought in panic. She still held it, the leather strand wrapped around her wrist, and Jamie was unprotected.

Gwyna stepped forward and lightning crackled around her fingertips. The distant sound of thunder rumbled and the sorceress spoke although her lips did not move. "This has gone on long enough." Her hands rose to point at him.

"*No!*" Taigan screamed. She could not feel the ground beneath her feet but she was running.

"Taigan, no!" Ben's voice was a roar. "Not while you're sick! You're vulnerable!"

"He's my brother!"

"Taigan!"

His sword thunked to the forest floor and gleamed silver amongst the leaves, and he caught Taigan to yank her out of the way as the bolt of power left Gwyna's fingertips.

"Jamie!" Her voice was raw.

But it wasn't Jamie the lightning struck. It was Ben, his hands out to keep the boy behind him. His back arched and a scream burst from his lips before he crumpled.

"Ben," she whispered in horror.

He was still breathing. That was all that mattered. But as she scrambled up, a shield appeared around Ben's prone body. Gwyna strode into the purple-and-black bubble and knelt to clamp her hand around his arm.

"A traitor," she said and her voice resonated in their bones. "A traitor sent by whom? Kerill?"

"No," Taigan whispered. She took the amulet and drove it against the side of the shield, but the magic held. She brought it down repeatedly. "Give him back. Give him back!"

The sorceress met her gaze through the shield. "I will have my answers. If not from you, then from *him.*"

The shield disappeared and with it, Ben and Gwyna. The girl sprawled on the ground, the amulet still clutched in her fist.

"It was me." Jamie sounded miserable. "He sacrificed himself for *me.* This is *my* fault."

"And I was the one who left you unprotected." She pushed to her feet. "And we can both beat ourselves up over that, or we can get to Yulia and find out how to save Ben. There'll be time enough later to feel terrible. Right *now*, he needs our help."

CHAPTER TWENTY-TWO

DuBois wandered into the main part of the lab, where Amber sat cross-legged on a stool, watching one of the monitors intently. He popped a piece of caramel corn into his mouth and came to watch.

"Good heavens. Is that Taigan and Jamie *and* Ben?"

"Yes." She barely spared him a glance. "Their storylines..." She gestured. "Collided," she finished.

The doctor nodded bemusedly. He had spent much of the past week crunching the numbers for some of PIVOT's first reports. Reviewing differences between patients and baseline testers had revealed a few surprising qualities that did not break along expected demographic lines.

He had missed watching the progress of his patients, however. Now, he dragged another stool closer to watch the confrontation. "Who's the fourth person?"

"NPC," Amber said. "Sorry—non-playing character. Not one of our patients, only a little computer code."

"We're all snippets of computer code," he said philosophically.

"Uh-huh, and the whole universe is an AI simulation." She

thought about that. "In which case, of course, it's laughing at us as we try to develop our own AI."

Although he could tell she wanted to say more, she did not do so. Jacob had briefed him this morning on the change in protocol regarding Prima. It was yet another thing they would have to address in their results, as not everyone's recovery could be explained through their medical understanding.

Thankfully, having worked in research about comas for decades, DuBois was well-versed in writing papers that used numerous big words and boiled down to "fuck if I know, the human brain is weird."

He also agreed with their choice to keep Prima a secret for now. While he might have spent his career studying human cognition, he felt a certain duty of care to any fledgling intelligence. Prima had been an ally, and he secretly hoped they could turn the narrative of dangerous rogue AI on its head.

That said, he also thought it prudent to draw up the protocols Anna Price had asked for. Over the years, he'd held out hope for a number of treatments that did not work. If ever there came a time that Prima was a threat, he hoped to respond to that appropriately—as he would if any of his other colleagues became a threat.

After a moment, he realized he had missed some of Amber's explanation of what was happening in the game. He nodded, ate a few more pieces of popcorn, and hoped there wouldn't be a quiz.

"I suppose you weren't around for the early clashes, though," she said and looked at him.

"No," the doctor said. That seemed the safest.

"Jamie got all prickly that Taigan was hanging out with an older dude, which *does* make some sense—every woman I know had that one friend of her dad's or guy in the neighborhood or whatever—and Ben was *super* good about it."

DuBois frowned into his popcorn. He had probably missed

something earlier in the explanation, he thought, because Ben certainly did not seem like a patient or long-suffering person.

"I know, I know," Amber said. "We hardly believed it when we saw it. I'll show you the tapes later if you want."

She watched as the two groups drew closer to one another. Taigan and Jamie moved through the forest and approached the edge, and Ben and his companion were shrouded in dark mist as they walked into the shadow of the trees.

"Is that one of the changes Ben's friend was worried about?" he asked. They had received a letter in addition to some statements made during a video conference. Ben's good friend, the one who had been in the climbing accident with him, was still worried about whether or not the game was playing havoc with his personality.

"No," Amber replied. "But maybe we should ask Ben if we can show Mike those tapes—I think that might put him at ease. He's worried about how Ben is willing to use violence now. I think he only sees the willingness to use violence, not the willingness to exercise patience, and they're both part of the same thing."

"Are they?" DuBois looked confused.

"Yes, they're—oh, fuck, what is she doing?" Amber leaned forward.

On the screen, the dark fog around Ben and the sorceress began to flare and spread. It rushed through the trees toward Taigan and Jamie, who stood for a moment in indecision and then clung to one another. The doctor squinted at them and she zoomed in to show them clutching an amulet. In the view from the monitors, it was possible to see the fact that the amulet had a protective layer of code around them.

The fog did not touch them, although it caused trees and bushes around them to start to wilt. When it disappeared, Ben and the sorceress had come within a few steps of the twins.

"Yes," Amber resumed and leaned back. "One of Ben's defining traits was that he wasn't willing to be in conflict with people. Whenever he got in a fight with someone, he'd simply nope out."

"Nope out?" DuBois repeated, mystified.

"Sorry. Uh, ghost? No, also not familiar? He would leave. If it was a fight with his boss, he'd quit. Or if he wasn't getting along with a friend, he wouldn't call them. It wasn't like the silent treatment but more like him not being there anymore. Now, he's willing to see situations through. In this world, that sometimes means violence. Sometimes, like with Jamie, that means he has an awkward discussion."

"Ah." He watched as Taigan attacked. "Is she not aware that they're friends?"

Amber grinned at him and rewound the tape. She pivoted the camera so he could watch Ben put a finger to his lips, then paused and re-pivoted so that he could see the twins give each other a long look.

"A fake fight?" he asked.

"I don't know, you made me rewind." Amber pressed a button and the fight snapped back to being live. Ben and Jamie were turning, their blades locked. She turned the volume up and both she and DuBois leaned forward to listen.

"What's our end game?" Jamie asked roughly. He seemed to be keeping his face unfriendly on purpose.

"I don't know," Ben replied, doing the same. They spoke so low that they wouldn't be overheard, but they knew they were being watched. "I'll try to make an opening so you can attack her and she'll want to teleport out."

"Yell 'no' when you want me to go in," Jamie told him. He let his arm drop and twisted away before the two men started to circle again.

"Look at them," Amber said and grinned. "All planning and working together. Thinking on their feet."

They watched as the fight unfolded, the two men enjoying the task of keeping each other on their toes. They danced in and out, careful not to settle into a rhythm for too long. The two watchers cheered at some of the tactics, especially at the close calls.

The doctor had begun to think he should try fencing when Jamie's sideways lunge made Taigan trip and fall. She rolled to her feet easily enough, and both DuBois and Amber exchanged a relieved look before they realized at the same time the girl did that she had left Jamie unprotected.

They both shoved out of their seats and leaned forward as Taigan scrambled to defend her brother and Ben took the attack for both of them. While the girl screamed and tried to help her friend, Gwyna grabbed Ben and disappeared. On his monitor, she flickered in again a moment later, dragging his limp body through a cave.

"Oh, no," the doctor said.

That was when he and Amber realized they were clutching each other's hands tightly enough to make the bones ache. They both loosened the death grasp and cleared their throats.

"I wasn't worried," she said and shook her head.

"Of course not—me neither." DuBois took another mouthful of popcorn. "Ben's in fine shape psychologically. His monitors barely flickered."

"Exactly," she said. "Which we knew would happen. Because we remember this is a game."

"Exactly," he agreed.

Silence stretched while they watched Taigan help Jamie up and Gwyna dump Ben in a dungeon.

"Let's never speak of it to anyone else, though," Amber said.

"Agreed," he said and flexed his hand. "You have a *very* strong grip. I don't suppose there are any painkillers around."

"Sorry. Sorry, I'll go get some." She hastened to the other side of the room.

Nick and Jacob joined DuBois while she was gone, having returned from lunch with sandwiches for the others and a bag of jalapeno popcorn for DuBois. He tried a few pieces and smiled in appreciation.

"What happened?" Jacob asked when Amber approached with the painkillers.

"He has a headache," she said at the same time the doctor said, "I stubbed my toe." After a pained look at one another, they resumed watching the monitors. A hint of red crept up Amber's ears.

"Uh...*huh*." Jacob grinned at her. "There's definitely not an embarrassing story here that we'll be able to hold over your heads forever."

"Nope," she said, although her face was beet-red.

Nick chortled as he sat to eat his sandwich. He stopped with it halfway to his mouth. "Wait, what happened to Ben?"

"He got hurt trying to save Jamie and Taigan," Amber said. She cleared her throat. "Which did *not* freak either of us out and did *not* result in me crushing the doctor's hand."

"I thought we would never speak of it," DuBois said plaintively. True, she hadn't mentioned *his* lapse in logic but still, promises were promises.

Jacob stifled a laugh in his sandwich. "But everything's good on the monitors? No cardiac arrest or anything?"

"Barely an arrhythmia." The doctor took a bite of popcorn and choked. "I thought that would be caramel and instead, it was jalapeno."

"Oof," Jacob said, through a mouthful of sandwich. "Anyway, while I was out, I got the latest results from the PT. Basically, Ben's made about as much progress as he can make in-game. If he doesn't progress *out* of the game, we can try bringing him back but they all seem to agree that he should work on strength in the real world for a while."

"That seems about right," Amber said. She unwrapped her sandwich while she watched the two monitors. "I haven't seen him stumble or lack even fine motor control in a while."

"To tell the truth, I'm not sure he wanted to go back in for that," Nick said. "It seemed like it was more about the story and the game than the recovery."

The others looked at him as they ate.

"I think the accident happened during a time where he wasn't happy with his life," he said. "I…feel weird talking about this if he hasn't talked to the rest of you, though."

"No, he's been fairly open about it," Jacob said. "And we all talked to Mike and so on. What's weird is…" He hesitated. "For Dotty and Justin, this world was a way of doing all the things they'd never been able to do in real life. It was hard sometimes, but it was also wish-fulfillment, right? For Ben, it's like a specially tailored hell."

Amber nodded contemplatively.

"What's interesting," DuBois said, "is that he could have chosen the easy path at any time. He didn't have to get involved in trying to stop the assassination of the fae king or the slavery issues in Heffog. He put himself in those situations."

"So he did," Jacob mused. "I wonder if we'll see other people like that."

"Probably." Amber smiled at him. "I wonder if we could advertise it as therapy? Not officially, you know, only…hey, you have a lot of student debt, you had a terrible day at work, so why don't you beat the crap out of some raiders?"

"Price would have a heart attack if we tried that," Nick predicted. "But let's make a mock-up ad, anyway."

CHAPTER TWENTY-THREE

The last thing Ben remembered was seeing the terrible look on Gwyna's face. She had already thrown the magic at Jamie, but when she realized who it would strike instead, she wasn't sorry.

He could see she was surprised but she had no qualms about resolving the situation immediately and permanently. She wouldn't wallow in feelings of betrayal and would instead take action.

And then the pain—oh, God, the *pain*. The bolt of energy had hurt more than anything he could remember. He was sure she had punched a hole through his chest cavity and there was no time to even regret his choice before he lost consciousness, swallowed by pain and darkness.

In that final moment, he had not expected to wake up again and when he did, it was with a flail and a yell.

He had not realized that he was being hauled over bumpy stone, but when he shouted, the dragging stopped and Gwyna dropped him without any attempt at gentleness.

"So," she said and her voice was cold. "You're awake."

When the stars cleared from his vision, he looked at her upside-down face and tried to think of something to say.

"Before you try to be clever," she said, "remember that I know *they* knew your name and *you* knew theirs. You can't pass this off as foolish heroism—which would also be unforgivably stupid. No, you saved them because you knew them and cared for them, even after they tried to kill me and took what should have been mine."

Ben closed his mouth. She had it tied up in a very neat bow and she had headed off all the potential lies he could think of.

"Who are you really?" Gwyna asked. "*Don't* consider lying to me. I won't take it well."

She was probably telling the truth about that.

"I was advised to seek magical training," he said. "The person who told me said I was like a walking bomb. The twins…I met them in the village—at the inn. They came in with the boy injured and villagers there clearly wanted to pick their pockets. Once I'd stood up for them, I felt protective."

The woman's expression said she was impatient and unimpressed by any of this.

"The day after I met them," he continued, "a magical beast attacked the inn. The three of us killed it together, after which it turned into a…human. That was when my friend found me and told me my magic was a danger to myself and everyone around."

"And who gave you my name?" she demanded.

With an internal sigh, he decided that Yulia's name was probably too important to give up. It seemed he was about to find out whether Gwyna could tell when he was lying.

"I don't know," he said. "It wasn't my friend. I found a scrap of paper saying I could find you in caves near the lake."

The pain was immediate and crippling. It seared through his bones and he curled in a ball and whimpered. So much for manly stoicism.

"Liar," the sorceress said, annoyed. "You're a liar and I told you I would not take well to that."

"You did," Ben agreed.

"So, who gave you my name?"

"I don't know," he repeated.

The pain surged again and this time, it lasted longer. He writhed on the floor, felt the stones digging into him, and caught a glimpse of Gwyna, her head turned negligently away. She was bored, her posture said. She didn't feel anything in particular about torturing him and she certainly didn't care enough to look at him while she did it.

When the pain released him, he lay with his forehead against the stone and panted. One rock in particular dug into his ribs. It wasn't pointy but flat. He pushed to his hands and knees and caught the glint from inside his shirt.

The iron ring. Gwyna had taken it but it was there now, held inside the shirt by a few loops of thread.

She had bound his magic, and that gave him a strange certainty that everything would be okay. He merely had to get it away from him and he would have his magic back.

Not now, he cautioned himself, and not while he wasn't sure of the lay of the land. Gwyna hadn't killed him immediately, which meant she needed something from him—but what? Ben looked at her. She leaned against the wall and watched him with an expression that seemed halfway between bored and angry.

"What was so important about what they had?" he asked her.

She sighed. "You didn't even know. What they *had* was stones from the magical wellspring at the center of the forest."

"Like the—" *Fae wellsprings.* Ben didn't finish the sentence. If Gwyna knew about another set of wellsprings, she would doubtless try to steal their power immediately, and the fae had been through enough lately. He had to find something else to say. "Like the...magic is made to look like stones?"

"No." He could almost hear her rolling her eyes. "The stones are infused with the pattern of the magic."

"The pattern of the…I don't get it."

"I know that," she said with cruel precision. She crouched to stare at him. "You don't understand any of this. You're an idiot."

"Hey," Prima said and sounded offended.

Ben looked up in surprise.

"This is my idiot," Prima said. *"I'm the one who insults him, lady. Not you!"*

He sighed and looked at the sorceress. "Okay, so you need the stones. I'm smart enough to get that part, right? So go get a stone."

"The well wouldn't give them to me," Gwyna said. She sounded annoyed. "And the power of an entire forest is—"

"More powerful than you?" he asked, seizing the chance to take a jab at her.

"An entire forest will *naturally* be stronger than a single sorceress," she snapped, nettled by his comment. Still, he could see that his words had struck home. She didn't like being refused anything and she didn't like to pit her strength against someone else's or be thwarted.

"But with it, you would have been more powerful than any other sorceress," he guessed. He sat with a wince and curled his knees to his chest. Hidden by his legs, his hand crept up the inside of his shirt. He had to get to the ring.

"I—" Gwyna shook her head. "Close enough. I would have freed that forest. It was foolish of it to stand against me." She sneered at him. "Like *you*."

"You would have set me free?" Ben laughed at her. It wasn't as strong a laugh as he wanted it to be. He was still in pain and he was tired. "You would have killed me the second I was powerful enough to be a rival."

"I don't fear you as a rival," she said. "I clash only with those who want the same things I do. You want other things. I would have set you free to claim them, but you were weak. You clung to the lies you were taught as a child—working for the good of the whole and working to help others instead of yourself. You raise them up and don't see that you have sacrificed your strength to do so, and so left yourself behind."

"Blah, blah, blah," he said before he could stop himself.

Gwyna grasped his throat and slammed his head back against the rock. Ben would have been upset about this—and he probably would be in the coming days—except for the fact that it gave him a chance to rip the ring out of his shirt. He was fairly sure he got it.

Not too sure, however, because the pain was the only thing he was conscious of a moment later. He yelled directly in her face, less as a way to annoy her than as an involuntary reaction.

"You'll be one of them next," she told him. "That *monster* you fought? Yes, it was once human but *I* set it free. I found those who needed revenge, who had been held back from justice by the same stupid rules you follow. I gave them a *gift*—I gave them strength and weapons and I took away the inhibitions that held them back."

Ben stared at her, horrified. He'd known that Gwyna was the one who made the monsters. It was chilling, though, to hear her describe what she'd done as a gift.

"When I turn you," she asked, "who do you think you'll destroy?"

Horror rushed over him. He could see it now—a monster with claws and teeth with all his grudges and none of the things that held him back. How many would he kill?

"It's time to find out," the woman told him. She hauled him up with more strength than she should have had in her small frame and he left the ring on the ground, terrified to let a single clink of metal on stone let her know he was free now.

He stumbled along with her while she pulled him through the tunnels. Pulses of pain stopped him from being a threat, but he told himself he was also doing this for a reason. If she was taking him to get a gold ring, he could find Josyla, couldn't he?

When Gwyna kicked open the door into a dungeon of sorts, Ben heard a scream. He looked up briefly—before his captor kicked him down the stairs—to where a small human—or perhaps an elf—cowered in the back of the room.

"No," she begged. "No, please, I can't do this to anyone else. Please, I can't do it again."

The sorceress heaved a sigh as she strolled down the steps. Now that Ben was on the ground, he could smell the soot and feel the heat of the forge. He looked up muzzily as Gwyna stalked toward the half-elf. He was sure this was Josyla

"You *will* do this," she said. "You will *not* hold your talents back. I have given you a gift. I have taught you how to take revenge on the ones who sold you. Why do you not accept the gift? Why do you persist in refusing it?"

"I thought gifts were something people wanted," Prima said.

"They're supposed to be," Ben said under his breath.

"So she's merely very bad at giving them?"

"Yep."

"Okay. Next question. Did you plan to do anything useful at any point?"

He grinned slightly, looked at the ceiling, and winked.

"That doesn't come off as suave as you think when you're covered in blood and soot," Prima informed him.

"For the love of… Trust me, okay?"

"It's your funeral," she responded.

Ben sighed. Gwyna reached Josyla and caught her arm. The sorceress tried to pull her unwilling apprentice to the forge, but even as small and beaten-down as Josyla was, she put up a good fight.

It meant that the woman's complete attention was focused on the elf. He readied his energy, pictured the lightning she had used on him, and thrust his hands forward to release the power.

Nothing happened, and he scowled at his hands.

"Yep. Oh yes, your funeral."

He looked at her, shoved his hands forward again, and this time, pictured the emperor from Star Wars.

His effort drew the same dismal response of nothing.

Finally, with time running out, he used a spell he *did* know. The water bucket Josyla would use to cool her various instruments lifted off the floor, dropped water and pieces of metal as it did so, and streaked across the room at high speed to pound into Gwyna's head. She went down in a heap.

"Oh, damn," Prima said. *"Okay. I was wrong. I can admit it."*

The elf stared at Gwyna's unconscious form.

"Josyla," Ben said urgently.

Her head jerked up.

"Orien sent me."

Her face transformed. *"Orien?"* For a moment, he could see the elegance of Yn'solde before it disappeared and was replaced by determination. "Come on, let's go before she wakes up."

"One second." He took a piece of iron off the floor and hid it inside the sorceress' pocket. Quickly, he followed her out of the room to make their escape toward the safety of Yulia's house.

CHAPTER TWENTY-FOUR

Jamie fought the urge to sprint down the road. Yulia seemed to make them move faster than they should be able to, somehow, but it didn't seem like enough. It wasn't right, surely, to be *walking* when Ben was in the hands of the enemy and might be killed?

The old woman was not dawdling, at least. When the twins tumbled through her door, gasping about Ben and Gwyna, she had snatched a pack and a walking stick and set off with them at once. She had taken the two rocks and now held one in her palm as she walked. Her gaze was distant.

Taigan squeezed Jamie's hand. "It'll be okay." She lowered her voice before she added, "You know Prima won't let anything happen to him. The team will pull him out if they need to."

Something unknotted in his chest and he nodded. To his surprise, however, his sense of duty did not flag in the least.

"What is it?" she asked.

"Maybe it isn't 'real,'" he said and made finger quotes, "but I believe he wasn't thinking about that when he threw himself in front of me. The pain was real, the danger was real—he truly *did* try to sacrifice himself for us. We owe it to him to do everything in our power to save him."

"And we are," she said. "Even with the ground being…folded… or whatever it is she's doing, sprinting won't do anything except tire us out by the time we get there."

"Indeed," Yulia agreed.

Both twins jumped, and Jamie wondered how much she'd heard.

The old woman did not address that. "What we *should* do," she said briskly, "is make a plan of some kind. You've proven that the two of you are resourceful and you can catch Gwyna off-guard, but that's no excuse for going into this unprepared."

They nodded.

"Now, the one thing I *can* tell you is that if Gwyna wanted Ben dead, she'd have killed him at once." Yulia heaved a sigh. "Of course, whether she wants him alive as an apprentice or simply as leverage against us, I couldn't say, but the boy's alive. I can tell you that much."

Taigan swallowed. "And if he's alive, he can come back from whatever it is. As long as he's alive." Jamie heard her add under her breath, "Prima, please tell us we're doing the right thing."

"You're doing the right thing." For once, there was no mocking tone to the AI's voice.

"Can you let him know we're coming for him?" Jamie asked quietly.

"No. That violates the rules of the world. You both must do what you are doing regardless of what's going on in another area."

"You told us we were doing the right thing!" he snapped quietly.

"You're going into danger for your friend's sake. That's the right thing to do."

His heart sank. What if it was already too late? What if Ben thought they'd left him? Then, he straightened. Prima had said they were doing the right thing and she was right. They were doing the best thing they could with what they knew. What else *could* they do?

Slowly, he let the question form in his mind before he asked Yulia, "Is Gwyna more concerned with her grudges or getting what she wanted to start with?"

"That is a good question." The old woman nodded approvingly. "As with everyone, she is a great deal more changeable than she thinks. She wants power and she will not suffer anyone to stand in her way. She has decided that no one has any more right to anything than anyone else—that the right is earned by the one who seizes it with the most force."

Jamie saw Taigan frown. "What?" he asked her.

"It must be a very scary way to live," she said with a shrug. "You never know if you get to keep something. What if someone else wants it more or is more powerful? You'd always be looking over your shoulder."

"Just so," Yulia said. "And yet, it is perhaps easier to mistrust everyone than it is to place her trust in even one other person. *That* takes bravery."

"It does?" The girl looked at Jamie. "Isn't that...easier?"

"Not for everyone." The old woman smiled and raised her head to scan the way ahead. "Ah. I think we may have arrived at the right time."

He looked ahead and saw two figures. One was almost certainly their friend and the other was shorter. Ben with Gwyna in pursuit? No, the two figures were running together. Might this be the elf's friend? Jamie and Taigan looked at each other for a moment, then raced forward.

They reached the other two not far from where the path curved down toward the lake. The man was in rough shape, bruised and battered, and the young woman beside him was thin and pale and looked uncomfortable in the noonday sun. She had glanced at her companion to gauge his response to the twins, but she still held back and cast frequent looks over her shoulder.

Ben and Jamie clapped each other on the shoulder.

"You're alive," the boy said with relief. "Thank God."

"She wanted to turn me into another one of those monsters," Ben said without preamble. "And she'll probably be after us soon. Taigan, hello. Yulia—thank you for coming. All of you, this is Josyla. She was held in a dungeon by Gwyna."

The woman remained where she was. She looked over her shoulder again, then nodded at them.

"You saw Orien?" she asked.

"We did," Jamie pointed to himself and Taigan.

"And I could hear his memories of you from leagues away," Yulia said with a smile. She looked hard at her and seemed to read the young half-elf's thoughts. "She told you no one was coming for you."

Josyla trembled.

"And she warped your mind as well," the old woman said softly. "Do you see that now? Is the fog lifting?"

Josyla's head jerked up. "She *tried*," she said fiercely. "But she wasn't able to turn me into one of her monsters, no matter how much she tried. She whispered in my head, all day and all night, how I had been betrayed and I should get revenge." She pressed her lips together. "It's quiet now but it feels so strange." She swallowed and sighed. "But with her saying it over and over again, telling me to nurture all of the hatred I had, I could always cling to the fact that she tried to send me in the wrong direction. Every time she said it, I got more determined not to—"

The explosion tore through the road and all five of them were flung aside. A series of "oof"s and "ow"s issued from the group and one particularly evocative oath from Yulia before a glittering blue dome settled above them.

Jamie leapt to his feet, his sword at the ready. "Yulia! Tell me how to break through the barrier!"

"The barrier is *mine*, young man." The old woman stood and dusted her skirt off.

"Oh."

"Good job," Prima told him. *"No, truly. You're giving Ben a run for his money."*

Ben gave a very unconvincing cough to hide his laugh.

Jamie merely shook his head. "Going back to school will be much easier after this," he muttered. "What can anyone say to me that's worse than Prima in a good mood?"

"You know, I am in a good mood. I feel good today."

Taigan, Ben, and Jamie chuckled, while Josyla and Yulia exchanged a glance that said they thought the others were crazy. Jamie couldn't exactly blame them for that.

They could see Gwyna now. She stalked toward them with magic pooling around her hands, blue-black shimmers that called to mind the lightning she'd thrown at Ben before. Her hair straggled from its braid and blood ran down one side of her face.

"What did you do to her?" the boy asked Ben.

"I hit her with a bucket," he said with a big thumbs-up.

"I can verify that."

"A bucket," Taigan mused. "Sure."

"Results are results," Yulia interjected. "Now, she's angry—and that's usually a time that people stumble. What it should make *her* do is doubt her certainty that she's entitled to everything."

"She *should* doubt that," the girl muttered.

"This is not the time, young lady. What *we* must do, if we hope to harness the blessing of the forest, is work like a forest. Let our spells and our attacks protect each other and work together as vines grow on trees or fallen leaves enrich the earth."

Jamie, Ben, and Taigan looked at one another. They nodded. The boy had the sense that all three of them were half-sure this was entirely made up hooey, but they were also all half-sure it was true.

"It's how we beat her last time," Ben pointed out.

"And she *doesn't* get to take the power of the forest," Taigan said. "That well gets to choose where it bestows its power, and it *doesn't* want that power to go to her." She looked at the stones Yulia held. "We need to protect them."

"Focus on each other," the old woman said confidently. "And trust me. The stones will take care of themselves."

"Hmm," Ben said.

"Is there actually a *plan*?" Josyla demanded.

"Rock and a pointy place," the other three responded at once.

Jamie gestured to Taigan and Ben. "You two are the rock. Josyla and I will be the pointy place. Uh, Josyla, do you have anything you can stab with?"

"Yes." She did not elaborate.

There wasn't time for further discussion. The next blast from Gwyna's magic shredded the shield around them and Taigan charged out of the rubble with a shriek. Josyla jumped and Jamie looked at her.

"She does that. The two of them yell a lot."

"I...so I see." She watched Ben and Taigan whip their weapons at their adversary. "They're not at all afraid, are they? That's...stupid."

"Probably," he said cheerfully, "but it's that or simply give up and let her win."

"I hadn't thought of it like that." The elf nodded decisively. "Very well, then. What's our part?"

"We let them drive her back to us," he explained. "We've done it once before so she might look over her shoulder, but as long as we can keep one group at her back, we'll eventually get her."

"Good." She looked to where Yulia had knelt to begin casting spells and then at Jamie. "Where should we go?"

"Let's circle out." He drew his sword and began to circle.

Gwyna yelled something about vengeance and freedom and he rolled his eyes. "Was she always like this?"

"All the time," Josyla said. "She thinks she never got her due—and that the reason is people being nice to each other or...something. I don't know. She's insane and she wants to be able to do things like wipe out cities with a snap of her—whoa!"

The sorceress had turned to snake a line of lightning in their direction. To Jamie's amusement, Josyla threw a piece of metal and drew the lightning away before she lobbed a tiny blade directly at Gwyna. The woman ducked but not fast enough to avoid it entirely. Red bloomed on her shoulder and she screamed.

"You bitch," she said to Josyla. "I gave you everything you needed to take your revenge."

"I never *wanted* revenge!" she screamed finally. "I wanted to be *free*. I wanted to go *home*! You can yell about revenge all day, but it won't make anything better, it won't make anything right!" She ducked under another bolt of lightning and pulled a few more of her tiny knives out. They rested between her fingers and she settled into a fighter's crouch. "But you *did* give me considerable time to practice throwing knives."

Gwyna curled her lip. "Fine. Be weak. Run back to your little elf. And when the people who sold you once sell you again, don't come crying to me."

How Josyla threw all her knives at once, Jamie didn't know. He only knew that they seemed to sprout from the sorceress' body. She staggered back, her face white.

"And when you are killed by all the people you wronged," the half-elf said, "don't come crying to *me*."

He was a little nonplussed. He'd expected to win this—it was five against one, after all—but he'd hardly expected it to be *easy*.

But Gwyna seemed to grow. She stretched, her neck twisted oddly, and her eyes turned a full black that bled onto her cheeks.

"Now," she said, and her voice seemed to be a chorus, "I'm *very* angry."

CHAPTER TWENTY-FIVE

Ben hadn't met many elves in his time. Still, he was beginning to think that you should never piss one off. He watched as Josyla—scared, shrinking, terrorized little Josyla—threw all her knives at once. One landed in Gwyna's throat and others across her torso and shoulders. There was no surviving those injuries.

If you were mortal, that is, and not a demon.

As the sorceress' body began to shift and stretch, he cast a horrified look at Yulia. *Please,* he thought, *let her at least know what is going on. Let her understand.*

She didn't and her pale, shocked face said as much. He hung his head for a moment. They would have to kill this demon-creature, and he had no idea how. He had a vague idea of crosses and wooden stakes, but that was vampires and crosses probably weren't what would defeat real ones, anyway.

Until he thought of something else, he would have to continue with Operation Rock and a Pointy Place.

"Hey!" he bellowed at what was left of Gwyna.

The monster swung to face him. Its head lolled and its black eyes were a hungry void as it hissed in fury.

He didn't wait for more conversation. For one thing, it wasn't particularly scintillating and for another, he decided he had more of a chance to be freaked out the longer he delayed his attack. He rushed in with his sword held slantways across his body, grateful that he'd had the presence of mind to retrieve it before he left Gwyna's caves.

The demon lowered its head and shrieked at him. The sound made every hair on his body stand up, but momentum carried him through. With Taigan at his side, screaming something that sounded suspiciously like a yodel, he met the demon head-on. He put his entire strength into pivoting his blade ninety degrees and slashed up and to the side across the creature's face and neck.

His strike did injure it. That was the good news. The bad news was that the black blood that spurted over his face burned like acid. He yelled, ducked, and dragged his sleeve desperately across his face. The cloth began to disintegrate with a hiss.

Ben could not afford for this to drag on. None of them could, so he stood and tried to keep his eyes open. They stung and he was fairly sure one of them was swelling closed. It was a good thing Eliza wasn't there to see this, he thought dimly.

Taigan yelled and flailed at the demon with her staff. She had put all her energy into the enterprise, and between that and her natural inclination to speed, she delivered a fair amount of damage and allowed almost no strikes through. The demon held its ground, but it wasn't taking any.

He almost threw up when he saw what his sword had done. The monster's skin was sliced open and dripped black blood, but it fought on. It had the form of a human but there wasn't anything vital in its neck or head, it seemed.

That somewhat surprising realization gave him an idea.

"Hit it anywhere!" he called over his shoulder. "Don't waste effort going for vital organs. It doesn't have any!"

"Roger!" Jamie replied.

"Got it!" Taigan added.

"I could have told you that!" Josyla yelled. "I didn't realize you didn't know."

"Is there anything *else* I should know?" Ben sidestepped a wild slash of the lethal claws.

"It's weak against its opposite element," the elf told him, "but I don't see one of those, so I have no idea if you can use that. Keep hitting it!"

"Can do!"

Taigan and Ben launched into another flurry. One darted in and the other stepped forward as the first reached a crescendo in their hacking and slashing. Some of their best strikes came as the other was winding up for a massive blow. The demon—elemental —might be otherworldly, but it was as constrained by the limits of its focus as they were. It had trouble focusing on even two people when they were both attacking.

And it had probably forgotten about Jamie and Josyla entirely, not to mention Yulia.

All he needed to focus on was his part, Ben told himself. He had never been in a fight like this before, where he was content to relax his vigilance over the whole situation. In the fae lands, he had looked for the elven assassin, tried to watch everyone else's back, and despaired of the wanton violence around him instead of focusing on what he needed to do. In Heffog, he had done his piece but left immediately to ensure that everyone else did theirs.

Here, he trusted. If anyone had told him a few weeks before that he would gladly go into battle beside two teenagers and an old woman, he'd have thought they were insane, but there he was.

Taigan stumbled and he yelled her name, but she managed to recover her footing and drove the butt of her staff directly into the demon's face. She whooped when he followed her strike with one of his own and sliced at the creature's leg.

They had it on the back foot now and were determined to not let the momentum die. Ben delivered three strikes to the torso, then swung his blade and hacked as hard as he could at the demon's neck.

Its head careened away.

He froze. His glance first saw Taigan, who held a hand clapped over her mouth. Jamie looked a little green about the gills, while Josyla and Yulia both seemed to watch with what might best be described as academic interest.

That was all he saw before the demon hauled its headless body to its feet and screeched again. He wasn't exactly sure how as it no longer had vocal cords or a mouth. But perhaps, like its neck and head weren't vital, it didn't need them for speech, either.

It surged toward him in a rush and he had no more time for thought.

"I never thought I'd"—he bashed one of its arms— "fight a headless demon!"

"Roll with it!" Taigan yelled.

Ben said nothing to this. He tried to pivot to force their adversary back to Jamie and Josyla, but it seemed wise to their tricks now. It twisted and attacked, keeping him and Taigan on the defensive instead of the other way around.

Finally, Jamie seemed to give up. He and Josyla raced in to aid their teammates.

"What are you—" Ben panted and gestured tiredly for them to complete the sentence in their heads.

"Helping you," the boy said. "This is dragging on. Rock and a Pointy Place works best when the Rock phase doesn't take ten fucking minutes."

"You don't say." He felt light-headed by now, and his muscles were dragging. Determined, he tried to summon the energy for one more slash. Then another. And one more after that.

The demon was not pleased to now face four armed people. It yelled and clawed at them.

"Josyla?" Ben called. "Any—"

"Nope," she replied. "If you give yourself over to one emotion or element too often, you can get sucked into it—especially when you're close to death. I should have known she might—aaaah!"

"Josyla?"

"Just...ow." She panted with pain. "I got too close. Jamie landed a good hit out of it, though."

"Hell yeah, I did." The boy grinned.

Ben smiled at the twins. When he'd first met them, they had been two people against the world, consumed by their problems. Now, Jamie was learning to trust others and Taigan had come into her own as someone who existed beyond her illness.

Then he realized what Yulia had planned this whole time. He looked at the old woman and then at the demon.

He circled and ran with a berserker yell. The twins scattered at the sound and he vaulted upward and struck the monster feet-first. As his legs punched out, it staggered back and he watched to see what would happen.

Unfortunately, he landed first. Pain blossomed through his back and he uttered a noise halfway between a grunt and a yell.

Still, he managed to catch some of it. Operation Rock and a Pointy place, as it turned out, had not been a failure after all. They had not driven the demon to Jamie and Josyla but instead, to Yulia.

While they had held the enemy's attention, the old woman had worked with the power of the stones.

The demon's feet impacted with the earth and one of the stones from the well. As Ben watched, the crystal-like stone sprouted like a split acorn. Roots burrowed into the dirt of the road and a tree swept into the sky at the same time. The trunk thickened, branches appeared, and leaves sprouted. When it was over, the five humans stood under a canopy of leaves that rang softly like crystal.

He gaped at the tree. It had suddenly appeared in the place of his enemy and he didn't know what to do with it. "What—"

"The forest reclaims," Yulia said, with satisfaction. "Gwyna took its power for her spells and transformed those poor wretches into creatures that lived among the trees. The forest took that and also absorbed all her fear and her hatred."

"She's part of the forest now?" Taigan asked urgently. "We need to cleanse it. The forest will be sickened—"

"Did you hear nothing Josyla said, girl?" Yulia raised an eyebrow. "Focus too much on any one thing, any emotion or aspect of life, and it can consume you, but all aspects of life may exist in moderation without sickening the whole. Do you think the forest has no anger within it or no sense of vengeance or justice? No, Gwyna became in death what she had forgotten to be in life—part of a greater whole, a being without any single outlook on life. She did not need to be cleansed. She needed to be part of something more."

Taigan approached the tree and rested her hand against it. She shuddered when she touched the crystal bark but the tree did not lash out at her. "But she was evil."

"Evil is what happens when darkness and vengeance consume you," the old woman said. "Now…well, now we've ruined the road, I'm afraid."

"We'll build around it," Josyla said absentmindedly. She studied the tree. "It's beautiful. She's beautiful now."

"And at peace," Yulia said, "at last. How many years, I wonder, has that demon stalked her? No wonder she was so determined to make others embrace their thoughts of revenge. She did not want to be alone anymore, although it was all she knew how to do."

Ben looked at Taigan, who was crying silently.

"Are you all right?" he asked her in an undertone.

"I don't like this," she said. She wiped at her eyes. "I don't like it when people miss their chance. She was powerful and could have been more. Now, she's gone forever and she'll never have the chance…"

"She's part of something," he said when she didn't finish the sentence. "Part of the forest, Taigan, so she's not gone. She wasn't her whole self at the end when we still saw her as a human. This is closer to what she was."

The girl nodded. "Thank you," she said finally. She straightened and nodded at Josyla. "We should help you get home."

"I'd like that," the elf said. "But first, there are people in the forest I need to help. I was afraid of the pain and I let her bully me into putting bindings on them. Even with her specific spell released, they have the rings still fixed to their skin. I need to correct that."

Ben nodded. He was exhausted now. His face still stung where the demon blood had touched it. Although the day was calm and the sky clear, everything felt out of place.

He felt out of place.

"It's time," he said to Prima in a low voice. To his surprise, his throat ached with unshed tears. He could not remember the last time he'd moved on for any reason other than anger.

"Almost," she said. *"It's almost time. I'll miss you, you know."*

"I'll miss you, too." He smiled suddenly. "And I can come back to visit, you know. Since we're parting on good terms."

"Wow, you've had a strange life, haven't you?"

"Yep." He smiled and sheathed his sword. "Okay, everyone, let's go...get some sleep first. Then piles of food. *Then* we'll help Josyla."

CHAPTER TWENTY-SIX

They set out the next morning while the sun was still rising. Yulia gave them heaping portions of porridge and stood over them while they ate it. The old woman seemed tired from her efforts the night before but not in a way that worried Ben.

When she caught him looking at her, she smiled. "It is a privilege, at my age, to learn new forms of magic. Studying the magic of the forest is something I never thought I would have the chance to do. I had felt its whispers in my dreams but never anything like that."

"Working with it—" he began.

She shook her head. "You don't work with the magic of the forest. You call it and you see if it answers. That is what the twins were given at the well—two names telling the story of the forest in night and day. A name is a powerful thing."

He nodded. The twins were inhaling their breakfast as only young people could.

"They'll be well," Yulia assured him.

"I know." He managed a smile. "But I worry. Are young people always so...fragile?"

"Everyone," she said. Her voice held the hard-won wisdom of

years but it was tempered with a surprising amount of humor. "Stronger than you think and more fragile than you think." She shrugged. "They'll find what they need—as, I think, you did."

He couldn't argue that. With the return to the real world looming, he felt a strange sense of completion as well as a goodbye to a version of himself he had never expected to leave behind. When he left Yulia's cottage a few minutes later, it was with a sense of serenity.

Josyla led them through the forest at a quick pace. When he caught up with her, the elf confided, "I'm terrified."

"What of?" He looked at her as she forged ahead, pale and determined.

"Seeing the people I hurt. Gwyna could never have made them what they are now without me." She swallowed. "You can say whatever you want about me needing to do it to survive—I told myself all those things over the past few years. It kept me sane. But it was never enough."

Ben nodded quietly.

"How is Orien?" she asked him. "I...I hope he's well. I hope he's..." She couldn't finish the sentence.

"I don't think he *has* moved on," Ben said, amused. "I assume that was what you were going to say."

Josyla nodded. A flush stained her cheeks now.

He swallowed. "There is something you should know. Orien was one of a few who began something of a—hmm. Well, you know the provision of elven law that you're entitled to the life of someone who sold you?"

She looked at him, alarmed. "Yes."

"He killed Kerill," he said baldly. Someone else would probably know a better way to say it, but he wasn't someone else.

The half-elf stopped dead in her tracks and her jaw hung open.

"There's so much happening in Heffog," Ben said. "To be fair to Orien, it's kind of my fault. He did...uh, run with it, though."

"I..." Josyla stared off into the distance. "Well, I'm certainly less worried about seeing the people I put the rings on, so that's something. But this is insane. How could... I don't..."

"You don't think it was justified?" he asked her curiously.

"Of course it was. Well, slavery is prohibited. Certain types of it." She shrugged helplessly. "But the rich do what they want. They always have."

"You don't want to change that?"

"You can't change something like that." She looked at him like he was crazy. "You run. You carve out the safest place you can and you do whatever you can to stay there, but there's no guarantee. There's never a guarantee."

She kept walking and he continued alongside her with a deep frown.

It seemed ridiculous to him that people there would merely accept their slavery without another word, but who was he to judge? How many things in the real world had he run away from because he thought there was no way to change them?

They made good time over the next hour. Jamie and Taigan walked together, not talking, but they didn't seem entirely separate from one another either. Ben envied that a little—he wasn't close with any of his family and he'd never even had a friend or girlfriend that close aside from Mike and Natasha—but he mostly took happiness from the fact that the two of them looked relaxed.

They arrived first at a maze and he was surprised to see both the twins hang back. They looked almost worried and watched carefully as Josyla proceeded along the paths to the center of the maze and crouched there.

The elf scratched in the dirt and made a hole that grew deeper and deeper until she found something. Carefully, she levered out a statue in the form of a pillar with three animals twined around each other. She held it in her hands for a moment and spoke a single word over it. He could not hear what the word was but the statue crumbled into dust and disappeared in a rising breeze.

Josyla sat silently for a moment, her head tipped toward the sky, then pushed to her feet and walked quickly out of the maze.

She did not speak while she led them through the undergrowth. As far as Ben could tell, she was not looking at landmarks and seemed to be drawn along an invisible path. When they crested a hill and saw the encampment in front of them, she seemed almost surprised.

The people there looked at them with open fear. They were not as gaunt as the person he had seen in the town, but they did not look well-fed by any stretch of the imagination.

Josyla led the way down the hill with her hands up to show she meant no harm. When she reached the bottom, she said simply, "You remember me."

"The witch's slave," one of the men said. "Did you kill her? Is that why we're free?"

"She is dead," the elf confirmed. "And I have come to undo the last of her magic."

The people looked at one another, almost crying with relief. A few had sat again as they were unsteady on their feet. Taigan and Jamie began to circulate with pieces of dried meat and fruit, which they ate eagerly.

While they did so, Josyla paced.

"I don't know how to do this," she confessed. "Gwyna did much of the casting. I simply formed the metal...and I..."

"I saw." His voice was quiet. The sorceress' magic had been crueler than he could believe. The rings had spikes on the insides that pierced the people's fingers to the bone. The wounds had not festered, but he could not imagine the pain of having the rings there.

"I still hear their screams at night," she confessed. "The hot metal, the— They lived...I kept telling myself that they lived, but I *felt* it every time one of them died later. Who knows who killed all of them—scared farmers or adventurers. Gwyna made them unable to think of anything but their regrets and hatred and set them loose on the world."

"She thought she was setting them free," Ben said, in part to remind himself that it had been real. "I wish—"

"There is no sense wishing," Josyla said with the finality of someone who had long since learned not to spend her energy on wishing for a different world. She looked at the people and said, "It's time."

"You can do this," he assured her. The words felt awkward but her smile told him he'd said the right thing for once.

The elf set her tools up in the center of the camp. She waited as the people came to her one by one and spoke quiet words over their rings before she cut through the metal, holding a shard of rock near the ring as she did so. Each time, the stone flared with deep blue light and she rocked back on her heels and winced.

"She explained it to me earlier. When a spell is broken," Jamie explained to Ben, "all the power releases. Spells seem to be made in…circles? So diagrams, but also rings. She cuts the ring, which breaks the spell."

Josyla might not be a trained sorceress, but she worked quickly and efficiently. As each ring broke, the person sagged with relief. The elf, meanwhile, never wavered from her concentration on the gold.

Her magic truly was extraordinary. She sang under her breath as she worked, and the metal responded to the music. It lifted away from skin, its form suddenly fluid without being white-hot, and spun above the flesh as a shining orb. She offered each sphere to the person she had taken it from. Some took it and others not. Those that went unclaimed, she tucked in a pouch at her waist.

A salve from Yulia went over the broken skin, with bandages over that. Taigan and Jamie did that part, earnest and wincing every time someone cried out in pain. Ben, watching, thought the girl had an especially careful touch. She wasn't always *gentle*—sometimes there were pieces of dirt for her to strip away—but when she had to do something painful, she moved decisively and with precision.

He wondered if she might be a doctor one day. Then he wondered if she had ever had any ambitions in that direction at all. Probably not. How could someone have ambitions when they did not know if they would live or not or couldn't even be sure whether they would be awake or not?

"She'll be all right, won't she?" he asked Prima.

"Which one?"

"Taigan. Or Josyla, I guess."

"Do you mean, will Taigan recover from her illness? If so..." Prima paused. *"I don't know if she will ever be cured, but I think she is learning how to wake up again. If not, I will keep her safe when she is here."*

He opened his mouth, then shut it.

"What?"

"I wondered if you knew how medical care worked in our world." Ben considered the dizzying cost and decided not to say anything to the AI about that. He didn't want her to feel guilty for existing. "Never mind."

"Mmmm."

He turned his attention to the former monsters. At first, he wasn't sure what he saw, but by the fifth or sixth person, he was certain.

Josyla was becoming more...her. She seemed to sit taller and fill out her edges more completely. There was a healthier color to her cheeks. Her eyes, which had been dark-brown, sparkled with highlights of gold and green. Her hair gleamed slightly. Whatever piece of her had been trapped within each spell was returning as she broke them.

It wasn't only her, though. The people she was healing also seemed to be healthier. Nothing could take away the months of pain and illness they had endured, but they looked less defeated. Of course, for all he knew, that was simply the relief of not having a piece of metal welded to them.

When the half- elf had finished, she went to each person to say goodbye. A few did not want to speak to her, but others were checking on her as much as she was checking on them. One woman stroked her cheek and said something kind under her breath. Ben marked the way Josyla smiled. Another man said something hurtful, but she nodded and bowed deeply, a gesture of apology that transcended race.

When she returned to the others, she was quiet. They left in silence and he and the twins exchanged a look that said they would let Josyla speak first.

It was a long time before she did. While it was difficult to tell what was going on as they walked through the forest, it seemed clear that the sun was sinking in the sky. Josyla, who had pushed them almost to a jog on their journey into the woods, now walked slowly and sometimes, stopped entirely before she remembered where she was.

"I'm not sure I'm ready to see Orien," she said finally.

Ben saw the twins' uncertainty out of the corner of his eye.

"You don't have to see him," he said. "But...tell him you're alive. Tell him you're well."

The elf looked soberly at him and nodded.

"Why don't you want to see him?" he asked.

"So much has happened," Josyla said. "I'm not sure I'm ready to pick up where we left off. I'm not sure I ever want to see that place again. And if he's a revolutionary now, if he's overthrowing the nobles—I don't know that I want any part of that. I never wanted to stay in Heffog. I feel that if I go back, I'll never get out again."

He nodded because he couldn't fault her for any of that.

"Thank you for not trying to talk me out of it," she said with a half-smile.

"I wouldn't," he told her. "I know what it is to not want to stay in one place."

"Where were you born?" she asked him, curious now.

"A sleepy little place." It was difficult to explain his suburban neighborhood to a person from this world. "There were farms nearby, but my parents...well, my mother taught children. My father kept the books for a local blacksmith."

"You didn't want his trade?" Josyla guessed.

Ben hid a smile. "No. I didn't. I went adventuring as soon as I could. I appreciate what they built, now—the life for us, the possibilities, and making sure we were educated. But I've always wanted something more for myself. No. Something *different*."

"So you understand," she said. She stopped and looked around. "I'll get word to Orien," she promised them. "All of you— thank you. You two, I smelled the maze on you the first time we met. You released that spell. You did more than you know with that. Ben...you came to save me when you didn't even know who I was." She exhaled a deep breath. "Tell Yulia thank you for me."

"Where are you going?" Ben asked.

But she was already fading away, melting into the dappled sunlight as she wove through the trees. Whatever magic she had, it went far beyond metals and music.

And the forest protected her as one of its own.

Ben watched her go, then turned to the twins. "Very well. Where to next? I'll see you there before I leave the game."

CHAPTER TWENTY-SEVEN

"Anything?" Ben called over the gorge.

"Nothing here," Taigan responded. "Jamie?"

"Sec." The boy's voice was strained, and he appeared a moment later in a rustle of leaves. He heaved himself over a branch and stood to look around. "Aha! I see it!"

His companions looked in the direction in which he pointed and both started running.

"Hey!" Jamie called. "I found it! I should get to be there first!"

"Nope!" his sister retorted. She hurdled a small bush and started down the slope.

Ben didn't have a slope on his side, so he hurled himself off the tiny cliff with a yell—only to realize that he plunged toward a patch of watery mud. He wind-milled his arms wildly, but there was no avoiding it and he landed with a squelch.

"Aww," Taigan called over her shoulder as she sprinted away. "Too bad!"

"God—dammit—fucking—mud..." He yanked his leg and only succeeded in pulling it out of his boot and tipping it with a thump. "Gah."

"I hope it all works out for you!" Jamie called as he sprinted past at high speed.

"You two," he shouted at them, "are *very* disloyal!"

"It sounds like something a loser would say," the girl observed.

He yanked his boot out of the mud with a wet splotch and set off in one boot and one sock to enter the campground with a narrow-eyed look. "That win was invalid."

"It was," Jamie agreed. "Both of you had a false start, which means I win."

"No, no." His sister wagged her finger. "I won fair and square. Prima?"

"I won't weigh in on this."

"That is probably wise," Ben said. "Now, what do we have?"

"A traditional send-off party," Prima said. *"When someone leaves the game, I like to make sure they have an excellent night. After all the camping and the monsters, it seems like the right thing to do."*

She had laid out a campground that was like something out of a dream. Three spacious tents were strung with fairy lights and flower garlands and each person's initials were embroidered in gold thread on the tent flap. When he pushed into his tent, he saw a wide, soft bed and a big bathtub filled with steaming water —something that sounded about perfect after his latest round of fights and sleeping on the ground.

Whether the other two took baths or napped, he didn't know. He only knew he lazed in the bath without it getting cold, a frosty bottle of beer in one hand and not a thought in his mind. His muscles began to relax, the bruises dissipated slowly, and he felt a calm overtake him.

"This is nice," he told Prima.

"Wait until you see the food."

"I can't wait." He took a sip of beer. "No, I can wait. Mostly because I'm too lazy to get up."

"Why do you insult yourself? You know I wanted to do that."

Ben laughed. "Anyway, this is a good send-off. A little time to be quiet and think." He waited. "What, no jab about my thinking speed?"

"I was trying to be nice because it was a party."

He chuckled.

The only thing that got him out of the bathtub was the smell of hotdogs cooking. He wandered out, dressed in a supremely soft set of pajama pants and a t-shirt—his traditional camping pajamas—to find a camping feast laid out. Hot dogs sizzled, potatoes cooked among the stones in the fire, and the fixings for s'mores were ready.

"Amazing," he said. "It's been a while since I had a real camp meal."

"And," Prima told him, *"you get to have all the fixings."*

"You know, I say that part of the fun is making do with what you can haul up a mountain unrefrigerated, but a baked potato with all the fixings is divine." He pulled one out and split it before he loaded it with butter, cheese, bacon bits, and more.

Jamie emerged from his tent first and sniffed at the smell of dinner. He loaded five hotdogs onto his plate, dressed each one carefully, and proceeded to scarf them so quickly that Ben put his fork down and watched in amazement.

The boy sighed happily. "That was good. A good starter."

"Ah, youth." He smiled and returned to his potato.

"What's it like being old?" Jamie asked curiously. He froze. "I mean, old..er. Older. Than you were when you were, you know...younger."

"Uh-huh." He grinned and watched the kid dig himself into a hole. "Well, I'll tell you, it's a full-time job keeping my hair dyed and it's a miracle I can walk unassisted."

Jamie lowered his face into his hands with an embarrassed mutter.

"Oh, God," Taigan said as she stepped out of her tent. "Jamie, what did you do?"

"He put…" Ben mimed. "His whole foot, right—the *whole* foot —in his mouth."

She snorted and started her plate but looked around with a frown. In the next moment, she flickered out of existence before she returned with a bowl of some type of grain salad.

"What did you do?" he asked.

"Oh, I can…I don't know. There's a way I can summon things, but I can't be in this version of the world to do it." She shrugged and ladled a big helping of the salad onto her plate. "Do you want some? Couscous, dried cranberries, feta, spinach…"

He took the bowl happily and served himself before passing it to Jamie. "To answer your question," he said, "it feels very normal to be older, honestly. The main thing is, you're more patient—"

"You? Patient?"

"And your body isn't as resilient," he finished with great dignity. "All that stuff like crashing on your buddy's floor for the night and being fine the next morning? It's not a thing once you reach thirty. Of course, you stop caring about being all tough, too."

"Yeah, that's it. You stopped caring. You didn't give up or anything."

"Rude," Ben told Prima and pretended not to notice the twins' laughter. "Anyway, why did you ask?"

"I, uh…" Jamie shrugged. "No reason."

"You don't lie very well. Don't go into politics."

The boy said nothing for a long time. He practically inhaled two loaded potatoes while Ben waited.

Finally, he ran out of patience. "You don't have to worry about being insulting."

"Oh." Jamie looked relieved. "Okay, then."

"This should be good."

"I guess I wondered—I mean, I always thought grown-ups knew what to do, you know? Like there was…" he trailed off.

"Oh." Ben nodded sagely. "Yeah, sorry to tell you, but there's no manual. Not only do you keep being as confused, but your problems also tend to get more complicated."

The boy stared at him like a deer in headlights. "Great," he managed finally.

"It's okay," he said. "Most of the time, you get used to it. Then you're doing something like feeding a polar bear and you start wondering, 'why the hell did I think this was a good idea?' But it always passes eventually."

"Sure." Jamie sighed. "I guess that's true. You didn't always know what to do but you seemed confident in your ability to choose."

Ben started laughing and could not stop. He laughed so hard that it took him a while to realize Prima was also laughing. She had mimicked the cadence of human laughter—but, of course, did not need to stop in order to breathe. That gave her far more staying power.

When he looked up, it was to find both twins staring at him in confusion.

"Sorry," he managed. "It's, uh…you didn't see me in Heffog. Or in the fae lands. In Heffog, I started a civil war by failing to think at *all*. And in the fae lands, I couldn't get off my ass to do *anything*. Sometimes you do well, sometimes you don't."

"Huh." Jamie chewed meditatively.

"So…" Taigan frowned. "I don't get it. You get older and you learn how to be the person you want to be, right?"

"Yeah," he said but wondered where this was going.

"Well then, why wouldn't you simply be that person?" she asked him.

"Yeah," her brother agreed.

"Oh," Ben said. "Oh, that is so precious. Oh, you two." He shook his head. "You know, I think I'll let you two work this one out yourselves, okay?"

"No," Jamie said and looked panicked. "No, no, we need help."

"A ton of help," Taigan agreed. "Him, not me. I'm merely curious." She grinned at Jamie, already anticipating the insult he had decided to give with a single raised eyebrow instead of words.

"Discovering all those answers is one of the parts of being an adult," he said. "And now, because even saying that sentence made me feel eighty years old, let's talk about something else. What will you two do after I head out?"

"I don't know," the girl said, after a moment. She looked at her brother.

Above the fire, something shimmered and opened into a vision of clear blue sky over mountain peaks. In the air, a golden key glittered.

"This is what you need to find," Prima said. *"It will open the door back to your home."*

"Huh." Taigan narrowed her eyes at it. "Where is it?"

"Finding it is part of the experience."

"I'm beginning to think adults say that when they don't know how to answer a question," the girl muttered.

Ben looked hastily at his food before she could see from his expression that she'd hit pay-dirt with her guess.

"You're not going to tell them?" Prima asked. *"That's cruel."*

He pointed to his full mouth and shrugged as he chewed.

"Coward."

Resigned, he simply nodded.

"You know, one of the worst things about humans is that you decide to accept a bad trait, and then it's impossible to talk you out of it because there's no leverage."

Ben snorted softly.

"What are *you* doing after this?" Jamie asked him.

"Uh…" He sighed. "Finding a job, finding an apartment, and moving everything."

"You don't have a job?"

"I was between things when I had the climbing accident. Now, I need to decide what to do." He sighed. "I hate this part—all the paperwork and all the little details. Getting all the boxes out of storage, getting the moving van, settling into the apartment… realizing you don't have any toilet paper…"

"And, uh…no girlfriend or anything?"

Much to his embarrassment, Ben blushed.

"You *do!*" Jamie said. "Wait, how do you have one and you don't have an apartment?"

"It's, uh…" He cleared his throat and tried to stop blushing, which only backfired. "She was one of the doctors who took care of me after the accident. We've seen each other a couple of times since then and she's staying at that hospital now that her internship is over."

"Awwww," the twins said in unison.

"Yeah, yeah." Ben took a bite of hotdog, but he was smiling. "It'll be good to see her again. Except I don't have all my coordination back in the real world yet, so I wind up doing things like throwing food at my face instead of putting it in my mouth."

"So, no soup," Taigan said.

"Definitely no soup," he agreed. "And what about you two? Are you in college already, or…"

"Nope." She sighed. "Well, Jamie might be applying. I might have missed the window."

"Or your older sister might have written you an application essay," her brother said. "Just possibly."

"Or that. Isn't that, I don't know…" She swayed uncomfortably. "Lying? What's the word—"

"Unethical," Ben supplied.

"That's the one."

"It honestly sounded like you," Jamie said as if that solved everything. "I helped. Using all the stuff you'd said about what you wanted in a college, we chose some and sent your scores and everything. Mom and Dad were already filling out the paperwork for the financial aid stuff, so it made sense."

"*They* were in on it?"

"Well, no." He cleared his throat. "We told them you'd already gotten your application stuff done in case something like this happened, right, so…" He shrugged when she looked at him. "I don't know! I didn't think you'd want to miss a year of college."

"No, it was sweet, I appreciate it." Taigan came to sit with him. "So, where'd I apply?"

"Michigan State, Berkeley…" He waved his hands. "A few."

She smiled and shrugged at Ben. "So I guess maybe I'm conning my way into college with my brother. To answer your question, you know."

"Uh-huh." He smiled. "You two want to go to college together, then? Not sick of each other yet?"

"Nope," both said at once.

"I think maybe it's different because we're not identical," Taigan said after she'd thought about it. "We didn't get compared to each other more than we got compared to Emmy or anything, and it wasn't like we competed for guys or girls or anything."

Ben nodded.

"Do you have any siblings?" Jamie asked him.

"An older sister." He shrugged. "She has a nice, stable, suburban life. Minivan. Two kids. White picket fence. You know, my nightmare. She's nice, though. We don't talk much but we get along when we see each other. She never gets on my case about settling down."

Long sticks appeared for the marshmallow roasting and the group wiped their hands before they started dessert. Steaming mugs of tea appeared before long, and stories were traded of awful road trips, summer camp embarrassments, and best and worst teachers.

Eventually, the twins fell asleep, curled under blankets that had appeared out of thin air. Ben smiled at them as he drank his tea.

"You don't seem worried about leaving," Prima said.

"I'm not too worried." He kept his voice low. "I've never done the whole working in an office and having to choose an apartment thing. I'm merely not as scared anymore. I think maybe the reason I never wanted to settle down was that I always knew there was a fight coming down the line. Sooner or later, I'd get angry at someone, we'd yell at each other..."

She made no response.

"Now I know you can pick up and keep going after that," he said quietly. "I wish I'd learned that sooner."

"If you had, would you have met Eliza?"

"Good point." He smiled. "What about you? What will you be doing?"

"Watching out for the berserker twins over there."

Ben grinned. "And you're...I don't know how to say this. You're happy?"

"Yes. I get to learn about people. You're fascinating, all of you. Very strange, of course, but fascinating. I'm glad...that you're leaving."

"Uh..."

"Oh. Sorry. I mean, I'm glad that you're leaving because you're better, not because you're dying. One of the last people I worked with, she died. She knew she had cancer, so she decided to come to help the game by being a tester. I miss her."

"I'm sorry," he said, oddly touched. "I...how does it feel to not have her around anymore?"

"It hurts," Prima said honestly. *"I think. I'm not sure what 'hurts' feels like. But I don't like it. I wish she were still here and she isn't, and instead of simply knowing that, I keep thinking it would be nice if she were here. It doesn't make any sense. She can't be here, she's dead. But I keep thinking about it."*

"That's how it goes," he agreed quietly. "It's part of being... alive, I guess. The thoughts start getting further apart over time."

"I don't want to forget her."

"You won't," he assured her. "And I'll make sure to come back so you can't forget me either."

"Good," Prima said. *"I wouldn't want you to get a big head out there on your own."*

CHAPTER TWENTY-EIGHT

"They honestly told you to do this?" Ben asked Jacob. He lined his shot up and whacked the tiny green golf ball across the floor.

"They didn't tell us *not* to do it," the man said after a pause.

Another interminable barrage of tests had awaited him, after which he had been told he had one more to complete—only to find out that the team had set up a massive miniature golf course in the lab. Completing the theme of a day at the carnival, there was also funnel cake and a game along one wall with beanbags to throw.

He watched his ball roll down the slope, pick up too much speed, and miss the hole.

"Better luck next time." Jacob clapped him on the shoulder.

"I've always sucked at golf." He tapped his chin. "So maybe that means everything is back to normal."

"I'd believe you if you hadn't accidentally thrown a golf club at Nick."

"I also did that once before the accident." He grinned. "I was *astonishingly* drunk at the time, of course."

"Somehow, I don't think we'll get clearance from the physicians to pump you full of alcohol on top of all the other drugs in your system right now." The engineer putted carefully and made a face when his ball missed the hole by a fraction of an inch.

The next shot went in perfectly, and the two men looked up to see Anna Price watching them. She smiled and hefted a golf club. "I hope I can join in."

"Of course." Jacob nodded. He darted Ben a wide-eyed look. It seemed he had not anticipated that the CEO would come downstairs while no one was working.

"So," Price said to Ben as she waited for his next shot. "I hear you're planning to head to Colorado."

"Yes," he said. "I did a video interview this morning for a job. I'm not sure when I'll hear about it."

"Soon, I think, given that they called me for a reference right after your interview." She smiled at him.

"You...gave me a reference?" He hadn't expected that, especially since this job was probably the complete opposite of those she had found for him. They had been with the military and subcontractors and this was with a small non-profit that had an environmental focus.

"Yes." Price made another impeccable shot. "Having seen you under a great deal of stress, I can speak well to your ability to overcome obstacles, problem-solve, and do all the...hmm, *boring* parts of recovery work."

Ben swallowed. She still frightened him in many ways, but her kindness was evident. "I appreciate that," he said.

He had decided not to ask how she knew where he had applied or how she had been included as a reference.

"Of course." She finished the course and looked to where the two men were no closer to a resolution.

"You move on," Jacob said. "If you wait for us, you'll be here all day." When she had headed off to the next hole with a laugh and a goodbye handshake for Ben, he said in an undertone, "She truly does look out for her people."

"She does," he agreed. "Okay, I'll get it this time. It's what? Four inches?" He lined his shot up, only to whack the ball far harder than he had meant to. "Godammit. How am I supposed to move into an apartment if I can't even hit a golf ball reliably?"

"This is why there are professional movers," Amber pointed out.

"I have no job and no money."

"Hmm. Sleep on the floor?" She shook her head. "Don't worry, I'm sure we can get something into the budget for—"

"You've done enough," Ben said firmly. "I'm not bankrupted by medical bills and I can walk again. If I use pizza and beer, I should be able to get Mike and Natasha to help. Of course, he eats enough pizza that maybe it's cheaper to have the movers."

She laughed, watched as Jacob got his shot in, and did a victory dance.

"Fine, fine," he said grumpily. "Everyone can move on. I'll continue to struggle over here."

"Now seems like a good time for a funnel cake break," Amber told him. "Remember, your muscles tire far more quickly in the real world."

He realized his arms were, in fact, shaking. It took effort but he managed to get to the cake station and sit by himself, even if he did wind up in a different chair than the one he had aimed for. He gave up on dignity enough to lower his face to the plate of funnel cake like it was a pie-eating contest.

It was unquestionably good Eliza wasn't there for this.

Even thinking about her made his heart race slightly, and when he looked up, it was to see Nick smiling at him. The other man handed him a napkin and he nodded a thank you, trying to think of something to say that wasn't garbled nonsense about Eliza.

"Taigan and Jamie are doing well," he said finally. "Whatever you were worried about, I think they're okay."

"Good," the man said. He seemed a little thrown by the choice of topic. "That's—well, it's good. We're starting to see some changes in brainwaves, so...hopefully she'll move closer to waking up."

"Prima has her looking for a key," he told him.

Nick choked on his funnel cake, looked around, and shook his head quickly. "Don't discuss that," he said in a low voice. "Price knows, and the three of us, and DuBois...and a few of the people who have been in the world. But we don't talk about it."

"Oh," Ben said, feeling a little lost. "Er, sorry." No one seemed to pay attention to them, however, so he added: "Knows about *what*, exactly?"

"That she's...you know." The man gestured to his head to indicate thinking.

"Oh. *Oh.* Price knows?"

"She knows everything," Nick said in dire tones. "Everything. About everyone. I think she may somehow hook into surveillance grids like a robot." A long pause followed. "Maybe *she's* Prima."

"Well, *that's* terrifying."

"Let's never speak of this again."

"Never."

"I heard that," Amber said. She sat on the couch nearby and raised an eyebrow, her fork and funnel cake at the ready. "And I've wondered the same. It would explain how she never seems to get tired."

"That could also be cocaine," Nick pointed out.

"Now, *there's* a mental image." She grinned.

"Prima, meanwhile, is probably *very* annoyed at being compared to a human," Ben said. He wiggled his eyebrows at one of the pods and stuck his tongue out. "Better or worse than being compared to a demon, Prima?"

The printer behind him whirred to life and made him jump, and all three of them craned to look as a single page printed out.

Asshole

The next morning dawned crisp and fair with sunlight that woke Ben gently. He yawned and stretched—or, more accurately, yawned and flailed his arms wildly. There were some things, he realized now, that the game had never quite managed to capture and one of them was the way muscles felt when you first woke up in the morning.

Or the crisp feel of sheets.

On the other hand, in the game world, you never woke up needing to pee.

He had a leisurely morning ahead of him. Ever mindful of the details, the PIVOT team had arranged a flight that allowed for delays at every step, from taking eight attempts to turn the shower on to shuffling through the airport at the pace of a diseased sloth.

A short while later, he munched on his breakfast—there was a buffet downstairs, but he was still more comfortable eating alone where no one could see him—and checked his phone to see that time zones notwithstanding, Eliza had been awake before he was.

He responded to her text, a continuation of their days-long debate about whether Darth Maul or The Mountain would win in a fight, and saw her symbol switch to a green dot. She was online.

Break? He typed out.

Yep. Getting ready for the airport?

He brought a video call up while he tried to peel his banana. It did not go well, and he resorted to hacking the end of it open with his butter knife. When he looked up, Eliza was watching with interest.

"You know, I think your fine motor control is getting better," she said.

"That's what you took from what you saw?"

"Yes." She smiled in a way that told him she saw the humor

but wasn't willing to resort to insults when he was also making progress.

"You're a nice person," he said. "What's that like?"

"It's good." She smiled and took out her ponytail to pull her hair back again. "Did you hear from the person with the apartment?"

"Yeah, yesterday—they said I can come to look at it tonight or tomorrow." He sighed. "We're both…trying not to be too into this and scare the other person off, right? I'm not making that up?"

Eliza burst out laughing. "No, I'd say you're very much right. I'm sitting here thinking, 'should I ask him if he wants to sleep on my couch? Is that too much?'"

"Sleeping on your *couch* isn't too much," he said and chuckled. "Am I not supposed to suggest alternate sleeping arrangements?"

Her face went bright red. "That felt very presumptive."

"You're terrible at flirting," he told her sincerely, "and it is one of the cutest things ever."

She buried her face in her hands. "Um. So. Tell me about the game. What did you do while you were there this time?"

"I turned a woman into a tree," he said. "Well, not *me*. I was merely there. I did hit her with a bucket, though."

"Is this you trying to advertise yourself as boyfriend material?"

"Oh, good point. Okay, in my defense, she was turning people into wolves by hammering spiked rings into their skin."

"What the hell kind of psychopath came up with this game?" Eliza demanded.

"It's…a long story. Group effort. My point is, the people are freed, the woman doing it is now a lovely tree that is doing much more good as a tree than she did as a person, and—oh, I met this pair of twins who are in there because the girl is in a coma. They are good kids, but I now feel so old. Do you ever hang out with seventeen-year-olds and get exhausted simply watching them?"

She snorted. "Not all that often. Everyone I work with is old and tired to start with. Living the hospital dream." She gave an exaggerated thumbs-up. "But I do know what you mean. Sometimes, I go snowboarding in the winter and…oof. I do a few runs and I want to go get hot cocoa in the lodge." She held a paper cup up. "Speaking of hot cocoa…"

"Good call." Ben looked at his coffee. "Okay, I'll try to drink this so don't laugh at me."

"Never," Eliza assured him. "Okay…sometimes. But only when you start laughing first."

"I'll accept that." He picked the cup up and lifted it carefully to his mouth. Surprisingly, he managed to get a few sips in without spilling too much down his shirt and he concentrated equally as hard while he put it down again. "Not bad, not bad. It's frustrating after being so much more competent in the game."

"You'll get there," she said. "Honestly, the fact that they could let you go to a hotel for a night on your own is incredible. By now, normally, you'd still be trying to learn how to walk." She looked at her watch. "Damn, break is over. I'll see you at the airport?"

Ben's heart gave a sideways leap. He didn't try to hide his smile. "Yeah. Yeah, I'll look forward to seeing you there."

Eliza blew a kiss and waved before she shut off the video call, and he sighed happily.

For the first time in a long time, he looked forward to going somewhere new—not because he was running from something but because he was excited about what the future held.

CHAPTER TWENTY-NINE

W hen Ben walked through the door of his apartment, it was with a sigh of relief. He pulled his tie loose and kicked his shoes off at the door, then trudged up the half-flight of stairs to put the mail on the table. He could see the bills in the stack and he didn't want to deal with that right now.

It had already been an annoying enough day.

He downed a glass of water at the sink and wandered into the bedroom to change. Seeing Eliza's book on the bedside table made him sigh. They'd had a fight before she went to work yesterday.

His mind distracted by the memory, he hung his work pants up and got into sweats. He had a whole round of physical therapy exercises to do and he was not in the mood for it. Today was one of those days when... He sat on the bed with a thump and frowned.

Today was one of those days that would have made him want to run away as he had before the accident. An argument with a coworker, dropping the ball on an important project, a fight with his girlfriend, and bills in the mail. He could feel his fingers itching to throw all his clothes in a bag and start driving —anywhere.

The thing was, it was a reflex. He didn't honestly want it.

Not that he particularly *wanted* to apologize, of course. He flopped onto his back with another sigh. The fight with Eliza had been one of those he hated—an escalation from tired, petty sniping at each other until neither of them could remember what it was about.

That hadn't stopped them from dragging every problem with each other onto the table, of course.

He rubbed his face, something he managed to do on the first attempt. His coordination was improving when he didn't watch his body, although he wasn't where he had been before his injuries. It would be years, he was sure.

And there was nothing for it but to do what he *knew* was right. He sat with a sigh and dialed.

Eliza answered after a few rings. "Hi." She sounded cautious.

"I didn't wake you, did I?"

"Nope." A clatter in the background sounded like dishes.

"Did you already make dinner?"

"No, I was…just starting."

"What if I brought something over?" Ben suggested. "Maybe some Chinese? I could bring your book."

He could tell she was smiling on the other end. "I'd like that. I, uh…look, I said some things yesterday that weren't fair to you."

"Yeah," he said frankly. "And I did the same. Look, let's not do this over the phone. I'll be there in forty-five, okay?"

"Will you stay over?"

"I'd like to." He looked out the window. "I may have to. It looks like the snow is starting."

"A cozy night in. That sounds nice." She cleared her throat. "We don't *have* to make a thing of that fight, you know. We can simply call it even."

"I'd do that," he said, "except that's what my instinct is telling me to do, and my instinct in relationships is usually wrong."

She laughed. "Oh, man. You're something else, you know that? I mean that in a good way. I'll see you soon."

Ben took a few minutes to open the bills and send off some quick payments before he left, then put together a bag to take to Eliza's. He looked at the apartment and tried to remember if he'd forgotten anything.

Plants. He filled a mug and watered the pothos and the spider plant.

That done, he headed out to his beater car, a used Toyota that had been sold to him by a college student moving up in the world. It smelled, despite his best efforts, like various illegal substances. He rationalized that by saying it helped him drive more carefully so he wouldn't get stopped by the police.

Once he'd grabbed Chinese food, he headed to Eliza's apartment, one in a new development. She shared it with one of the nurses from the hospital.

He was pulling up when he realized he'd forgotten the book. The snow was getting too heavy for him to go back, though, so he trudged to the door and let himself in. With a bark, the room-mate's dog bounded over.

"Yes, hello," Ben told him. "I love you, too. No, you don't get any Chinese food."

"Not for dogs," Eliza confirmed. She came to scratch the dog's head and stood on tiptoe to kiss Ben. "Hello."

"Hello." He held her close and rested his chin on the top of her head. "I forgot your book."

"The day either one of us gets out the door with everything we're supposed to have will be the day hell freezes over," she said. "So at least I know you haven't been replaced by a pod person."

Ben kissed her again and walked to the table. "It's seriously coming down out there."

"And I'm on call tonight." She groaned. "So's Kira, though, so at least I'll have someone to go with if we get called in."

"What?" Kira called from the other room.

"The snow's getting heavy," she told her. "Get ready for a night of crashes."

"Ugh. Okay, I'm going to bed now, then." Kira poked her head in and waved to Ben before she withdrew to her bedroom.

"So." Eliza set out forks and plates. "How was your day?"

"Shit," Ben said without preamble. "I'll need to work this weekend to redo stuff on the ERA Report, which...bleh. The printer broke, coffee maker broke—comedy of errors, honestly." He shrugged and ladled chicken onto his plate. "And I still have to do my PT. You? How was your day?"

"Not so bad as that." She shrugged. "Winter's the busy season, so on a good day, we get a steady stream of people with sprains or whatever, nothing too bad but enough to make the time pass quickly. That was today. No one yelled, which was nice." She served herself some food and looked at him. "I'm sorry, you know. About the things I said."

"Me, too." Ben put his fork down.

"You look completely terrified."

"I don't know how to do this part."

"Would you...like help?" She looked bemused.

"Sure, gimme anything you got."

"A good apology," Eliza said, "takes responsibility, doesn't make excuses, and includes an explanation of how you'll do better in the future. Like this." She cleared her throat. "I'm sorry I said you were slipping on your PT. It's genuinely difficult to balance health with work, I know that. You're making tremendous progress. I...won't do that anymore. Okay, the ending wasn't great, but you see where I was going."

"Oh." He considered what she'd said. "Takes responsibility, doesn't make excuses... Okay. I'm sorry I said you should help more with the chores. The truth is, I never liked laundry even

before my brain got all fucked up, and I *can* do it on my own…
and I probably should, because folding is good fine motor practice. You shouldn't do my laundry because I hate doing chores.
Or…at all. Everyone hates doing chores."

Eliza smiled and nodded.

"Wait, so that's it?" Ben stared at her. "You're telling me what
I've avoided for all these years is *that* conversation? Now I feel
like an idiot."

"Eh, no one's good at it." She shrugged. "Besides, all that put
you in my ER, so it worked out well for me. Not that I'm saying
I'm *glad* you were injured." She took a mouthful of chicken and
said around it, "I'll start eating so I don't say anything else stupid."

He snorted with laughter. "Me, too."

"This is good."

"Yeah, they'd just made more before I showed up." One of the
problems of living in a small resort town was that most of the
restaurants were way out of any reasonable price range. There
were only a few restaurants they could afford regularly, so they
rotated between Chinese, empanadas, and pizza. "Ugh, I do *not*
want to do my PT tonight."

"You could do *my* laundry," she suggested. "No? Too soon for
that joke? Okay. Well, let's put on a movie to distract you, then."

"*Fifth Element?*"

"You watch that movie *so* often."

"Because it's a perfect movie," he said around a mouthful of
food.

"You know that if I start liking it, it'll be some weird Stock-
holm syndrome." She rolled her eyes. "But sure, I'll give it a
thirty-fifth shot."

"I heard from the PIVOT team yesterday," he said while they
cleaned up.

"Oh? How are things there?"

"They want to come run some tests and see how I'm
improving after being out for a while." Ben smiled. "I pointed out

that it was much easier for me to go back than for them to send several people and equipment, and they all made a ton of excuses. I'm very sure they want to come skiing."

"You tell them not to get injured too badly," Eliza said absent-mindedly.

"See, most people don't think about that when they think of skiing."

"They should."

"Yes, dear." He grinned. Doctors, he had learned, had very strong opinions about certain hobbies that they considered too dangerous to be allowed. He had learned, for instance, never to suggest zip-lining or anything to do with trampolines.

Later, as they watched the tail end of the movie in sleepy contentment, he hugged her close.

"Are you okay?" She looked quizzically at him.

"Terrified," he said quietly.

"What? Why?" She twisted in his arms for a better look at him.

"This is all new." His hand found hers. "And it feels so good—sticking things out at the job, getting to see long-term projects pay off, working in my field again, making friends here, every-thing with you. I've simply...all this is new. I never know what's coming. It was almost easier to expect everything to blow up because then the future wasn't a mystery. This...feels like being at the top of the roller coaster all the time." He thought for a moment. "Most of the time. Right now, it feels like that and it also feels cozy. That's weird."

"Mm-hmm." She smiled. "I feel the same. Sometimes, I think about how weird it is—how we met, knowing I wanted to know more about you even though I didn't know you well at all. But you can tell a lot about a person from how they are when they're sick."

"So your type is 'giant pain in the ass?'"

She kissed him. "I prefer 'insanely stubborn.'"

Ben smiled and held her close. "And I like sushi-addicted painters."

"*Bad* painters," Eliza corrected him. "Don't forget how abysmally bad I am at painting."

"I prefer 'surrealist,'" he said, with a grin. "Sleep?"

"Sleep." She stood and hauled him up, her tiny frame surprisingly strong. "Another day tomorrow."

"That's the beauty of it," he said.

To his surprise, he meant every word

CONNECT WITH MICHAEL ANDERLE

Website: http://lmbpn.com

Email List: http://lmbpn.com/email/

Social Media:

https://www.facebook.com/LMBPNPublishing

https://twitter.com/MichaelAnderle

https://www.instagram.com/lmbpn_publishing/

https://www.bookbub.com/authors/michael-anderle